YO-ABJ-514

PENGUIN BOOKS

THE HOUSE OF BILQIS

Azhar Abidi is the author of the novel *Passarola Rising*. He has been published in *SouthWest Review*, the Australian literary journal *Meanjin*, and *The Best Australian Essays 2004*. He was born in Pakistan and lives in Melbourne, Australia.

THE
HOUSE
OF
BILQIS

AZHAR ABIDI

PENGUIN BOOKS

PENGUIN BOOKS

Published by the Penguin Group
Penguin Group (USA) Inc., 375 Hudson Street, New York, New York 10014, U.S.A.
Penguin Group (Canada), 90 Eglinton Avenue East, Suite 700, Toronto,
Ontario, Canada M4P 2Y3 (a division of Pearson Penguin Canada Inc.)
Penguin Books Ltd, 80 Strand, London WC2R 0RL, England
Penguin Ireland, 25 St Stephen's Green, Dublin 2, Ireland (a division of Penguin Books Ltd)
Penguin Group (Australia), 250 Camberwell Road, Camberwell,
Victoria 3124, Australia (a division of Pearson Australia Group Pty Ltd)
Penguin Books India Pvt Ltd, 11 Community Centre, Panchsheel Park, New Delhi – 110 017, India
Penguin Group (NZ), 67 Apollo Drive, Rosedale, North Shore 0632,
New Zealand (a division of Pearson New Zealand Ltd)
Penguin Books (South Africa) (Pty) Ltd, 24 Sturdee Avenue,
Rosebank, Johannesburg 2196, South Africa

Penguin Books Ltd, Registered Offices:
80 Strand, London WC2R 0RL, England

First published in Australia under the title *Twilight* by The Text Publishing Company 2008
First published in the United States of America by Viking Penguin,
a member of Penguin Group (USA) Inc. 2009
Published in Penguin Books 2010

1 3 5 7 9 10 8 6 4 2

THE LIBRARY OF CONGRESS HAS CATALOGED THE HARDCOVER EDITION AS FOLLOWS:
Abidi, Azhar.
The House of Bilqis / Azhar Abidi.
p. cm.
ISBN 978-0-670-01941-0 (hc.)
ISBN 978-0-14-311657-8 (pbk.)
1. Mothers and sons—Fiction.   2. Culture conflict—Pakistan—Fiction.   3. Domestic fiction.   I. Title.
PR9619.4.A25H68 2009
823'.92—dc22   2008029021

Printed in the United States of America

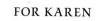
FOR KAREN

Listen to this reed how it complains:
it is telling a tale of separations

—Jalal al-Din Rumi
"The Song of the Reed"

PART 1

DINNER WAS SERVED at eight o'clock.

Bilqis Ara Begum, matriarch of the Khan family, cast a contented look around the table. Her brother and sister, her niece, her son and his new wife were all sitting there, waiting for her to say the benediction, the Bismillah: "Praise be to Allah, the Compassionate, the Merciful." She said it in a whisper, a furtive, almost bashful gesture of faith, and the family fell silent, concentrating on their meal. Bilqis had ordered her servants to cook a bhujia with spinach and potatoes, a kofta dish, kebabs, a chicken curry and another bhujia with okra. The kebabs were laid out on a white china platter in the center of the table. The rest of the food was served in beaten brass bowls to keep it warm.

The Khan family had gathered for the wedding reception of Bilqis's son, Samad, who had recently married an Australian girl of European descent. The wedding itself had taken place in Melbourne, but the couple had flown to Karachi to give Samad's family in Pakistan a chance to meet the bride. Mahbano, Bilqis's sister, and her husband and daughter had flown in from Lahore and Bilqis's brother, Sikander, who had rooms at the Sind Club, had driven over in his old white Mercedes. It was March 1985, and spring was nearly at an end. The reception was in two days' time.

Bilqis presided over the table with a sovereign but kindly air. She watched the guests as they ate, and coaxed and cajoled them if they resisted. The last rays of the sun, streaming in through the window, emphasized her Mughal features—the small mouth and chin of her aristocratic mother, and the high cheekbones, hooked nose and long, arched eyebrows of her father. She was a tall and elegant woman in her late sixties. She wore a white shalwar kameez, her hair was gray, swept back and held by pins. She had stopped dyeing it when her husband passed away. Her skin was fair and slightly freckled. The backs of her hands showed a web of veins. Her wrists were small, delicately fashioned, and her fingers long like those of an artist or a pianist. The way she held up her head, her straight back, her gestures, the way her stern face broke into a smile—all these expressions, at once light and graceful, and quite without affectation, hid successive generations of breeding. They were not so much acquired as inherited, and as much a part of her fiber as flesh and bone. But if they revealed the origins of her patrician forebears, they also concealed a conservative streak, a moral pride that the turbulent times had transformed into an inflexibility of manner, a disdain for change and a nostalgia for lost glory.

The enormous chandelier hanging over the table gave her dining room an imposing and rarefied air, but its light was dim and the old Empire furniture in the adjacent drawing room was already lost in the shadows, mute witness to the hunting scenes on an immense Persian carpet, where tigers and deer had come to life and were fleeing the arrows of a handsome archer, who galloped serenely on horseback across a meadow strewn with flowers. A narrow glass table was cluttered with family photographs in silver frames, which occasionally included a famous face, here a politician, there an author, all gone now, scattered to the winds. The shadows also camouflaged signs of decay. The once-springy carpet was balding in patches and there was dust inside the mahogany-and-glass cabinet that held captive a Dutch flower girl, missing her porcelain arm from when some servant, lost in a daydream, had let her slip out of her hands.

Bilqis turned to Zainab, her niece. Mahbano's daughter was a cheerful young woman with sparkling eyes. She wore a black shalwar kameez of her own design, the lines of her dress long and flowing. The subdued colors drew out her fair skin, the thin waist highlighted her tall, slim figure. "You must eat, my dear," Bilqis said in an affectionate tone reserved for indulging children. "Don't misunderstand me, but you look a little anemic. What are you afraid of? I oversaw the cooking myself. Not that one should eat to excess, but you barely touched anything. What, do you mean to refuse me?"

Zainab relented but Bilqis gave the recalcitrant a final glance, a rejoinder and an acquittal. A fine girl, she was thinking, as she ladled out the chicken curry on her plate. Why had her son not married her? Such marriages strengthened families and kept them together. Their children would have been beautiful, the match perfect, mending bridges and settling scores. It was just one more of her dashed hopes, misplaced and improbable. Marrying cousins was no longer in fashion, Bilqis reflected. People would frown upon it. A first cousin was like a sister to Samad. The relation was too close, too familiar. And besides, it was too late.

Zainab's nemesis sat next to her. The girl's name was Kate. She had brown shoulder-length hair. She had painted her nails and wore lipstick, but her makeup was subtly done. If she had any blemishes, they were not visible. She looked older than Samad, although she was a few years younger. Western women always looked older than their age, Bilqis thought. She looked at the gentle swell of her chest, the line of her nose, the chin and the eyes and the distance between them—all these details were inspected for the hundredth time. She was outspoken and a little too confident, attributes that were not becoming in a daughter-in-law, but at least she was not presumptuous. She was genuine and courteous. She thanked the servants each time they brought her something. To please her mother-in-law, she wore bangles and had plaited her hair in a braid. Slim and attractive, she looked at everything with curiosity, like a child. Bilqis was quite taken by the girl's charm, but her concerns had not been excised from doubt. From time to time, old prejudices emerged from the shadows. The girl was pretty, but there was something incongruous about this prettiness, as if she were a succubus in disguise. History was littered with tales of foreign sirens who had ruined good men. Had Cleopatra not rolled at Caesar's feet, he might not have died on the stairs of his Senate. And were not the fires that raged in the Middle East lit when Delilah lay with Samson?

"I remember the last time I came, there was a badam sapling in your driveway," Mahbano said to her sister. "It's not there anymore. What happened to it?"

"It's still there," Bilqis said. "I had it replanted next to the plum tree, because it gets more sunlight there. You can see it from the drawing room."

Kate listened to the conversation with relative ease. The family conversed in English for her sake. Sometimes they lapsed into Urdu, but there were so many English phrases thrown into their speech that she understood generally what was being said.

"What's a badam tree?" she asked.

"An almond tree, if you like," Bilqis said. "Almonds do not grow in Karachi, so badam is actually a misnomer. It's a wild unnamed fruit that grows on that tree, like the green fruit that grows on my Virginia creepers along the side of the house. They look like grapes, but they aren't grapes. You should never eat them."

"I love it when the blossoms come out," Mahbano said.

"Would you like to take some seedlings back with you? There's a nursery I know that's not far away. I could arrange for the chauffeur to drive you there."

"You make it sound all too easy."

Bilqis allowed herself a pause, knowing that after hiring and dismissing a number of gardeners Mahbano had taken up the spade herself. Her sister's hobbies never lasted long. "You'll need manure," she said.

Mahbano was eight years younger than her sister and looked more youthful than her age. She liked telling people that living in Lahore had kept her young. Lahore had everything going for it, charm, culture, architecture—white Mughal minarets, pink Edwardian façades and, once out of the city, orchards of orange trees and checkered fields of green and gold all the way along the Grand Trunk Road to the foothills of the Himalayas. The town of Murree, the old hill station of the Raj, was a day's drive away. One could leave the seething plains in the morning and wake up to the sight of snow on faraway peaks the next. Where could one go in Karachi except to the beach, where the water was like mud?

"Young Chambeli performed at the Alliance Française last night," Sikander remarked. "The whole of Karachi is rushing to see her. It is an open-air show under the stars. The mosquitoes suck you dry but everything is hush-hush and clandestine, which makes it exciting. I half expected the police to barge in at any moment and bust us. You should go before the mullahs put a ban on it. They will come around to it sooner or later."

Bilqis wondered if he had a drink before dinner. She tried not to smile at his fondness for dance, and for whiskey, of which she disapproved. "I used to see the girl dance when she was a child," she said. "Her mother was known to me, you know, but courtesans of those days were not what they are now. The fault does not lie with them. It lies with the times, of course. She is delicate and has the good taste and impeccable manners of her mother. She charmed you?"

"Well, at my age and with my vices, all daughters of Eve look charming. I was perfectly enchanted!" said Sikander good-humoredly. He was the middle sibling, a tall, straight-backed man with a thin mustache who retained a passing likeness to the graying Clark Gable. He was dressed in a white short-sleeved shirt and wore smart khaki trousers. A graduate of the Indian Military Academy, he had fought with the British Indian Army in Italy and Burma during the Second World War but resigned his commission after the Partition of India in 1947. A journalist of some repute, he had never capitalized on his looks or his fame. It was a matter of ever-lasting dismay for Bilqis that he had remained a bachelor, but he was a content and happy man. He played cards with his friends, drank a little and pounded away his regular columns for *The Dawn* on a typewriter. Marriage would have intruded on his habits.

"Well, there is something to look forward to," Bilqis remarked, turning to her sister. "I haven't seen her performance yet, but she learned kathak at her mother's feet. She dances very well. You need an outing. I'll take you if your husband doesn't. We don't want him to suffer for our sins now, do we?"

The sting in this last remark was meant for Shahid, her brother-in-law, who was late for dinner, as he had been offering his prayers in a room upstairs. A stout man, he now waddled across the room in his starched white shalwar kameez, with feet splayed and meaty arms rowing by his side as he took his seat between Sikander and Zainab.

"Did I hear someone mention me?" he asked, glancing around the table.

"My sister was suggesting that you might take me to a dance," Mahbano said.

"Then I will, of course."

"But do you approve of it?" Bilqis asked.

"If you approve, then how can I disapprove?"

"Oh father!" Zainab groaned.

"Now don't be waylaid by these women, Shahid," Sikander said. "If you go to hell for their sake then who's going to plead for sinners like me?"

Bilqis watched Shahid plunge with zest into his plate of koftas. He rolled up his sleeves, murmured, "Bismillah," and began eating with the proprietary air of someone who knows that his star is rising. It was widely known that in a few months he would become a member of the Provisional Assembly and in a few years he would be a minister in the straw parliament that the stone-faced newsreader on the state-run television station insisted on calling the National Assembly.

Bilqis did not doubt his piety, but she had to avert her eyes from his face, where there had materialized the characteristic callus that comes from the Muslim practice of prostrating the forehead onto the ground five times a day. A lifetime of prayers was usually required for the callus to appear, although in his case, it had already arrived in middle age. Not that there was anything untoward in its appearance. After all, didn't the Irish nuns at Loreto House teach her long ago how the stigmata manifested themselves on the bodies of saints overnight? It seemed still quite a coincidence that beards, bruises and other hallmarks of piety were appearing among the populace at the same time as mullahs were rising to power.

Old resentments rose and clutched at Bilqis's heart. Mahbano's was a love marriage, something that Bilqis had always looked upon with disfavor. Shahid came from feudal Punjabi stock, with generations of farmers and village headmen going back into the proverbial mist. His elders could neither read nor write. They used thumbprints as signatures and invented a family name because official

forms required one. Bilqis had expected that the differences in class
and upbringing would lead to a tumultuous marriage instead of the
seemingly untroubled union that it was. Of course, one could never
know for certain the truth that lay behind any marriage. Mahbano
was not unhappy, which is not the same as being happy, but it is
better than being downright miserable; and as for Shahid, well, the
marriage had civilized him, admitted him into society and made
him powerful. The sisters had made their peace long ago, but occasionally Bilqis could taste the crow she had eaten, and then she
would remind herself that the matter was forgiven—forgiven, yes,
but not quite forgotten, for Shahid had married outside his proper
station, married a woman with a considerable dowry, in fact, and
earned himself a place in society that no amount of money could
ever buy.

"The kebabs are marvelous," Shahid remarked, licking his fingers, and making a sign to his wife to pass him the white platter for
another helping. "If I succumb to gluttony tonight, then let it be
known that the fault lies not with me. It lies with the hostess," he
added, glancing at Kate. He spoke bad English with confidence.

"But I did not cook them," Bilqis replied.

"You have a superb cook then," Shahid said, without missing a
beat. "I cannot tell the difference."

The process of gentrification, Bilqis could see, had begun. It
was in its infancy, as he still had a boisterous manner suggestive
of underlying coarseness, but all the same Bilqis did have regard
for him as a result of all the favors he had done for her. He managed her affairs. He protected her from red tape. Whether she
needed a new passport or a visa to travel overseas, he arranged
everything without asking for anything in return, but each favor
was a validation of his power, which corresponded to a decline of
her own, and so she had to display a certain indifference. She

made a show of punctiliously fussing over the fork and spoon that Mumtaz, the servant girl, had scattered carelessly around her plate, but she was pleased by the compliment. She had decided which dishes were to be prepared, tasted the food and mixed the spices, but Mumtaz had prepared the dinner and, for once, she had done it nicely.

The girl came into the room bringing a bowl of rice. Shahid said a few complimentary words to her in Urdu, nodding at the food with his chin. Mumtaz looked at Bilqis in acknowledgment, as if the compliment and gratitude belonged to her, and returned to the kitchen without saying anything. She was pretty, slender and dark. Her black hair was tied in two long braids.

"'Delicious meal,'" Samad translated at Kate's side. "'Well done!'"

"That's Hameeda's girl, isn't it?" Mahbano asked.

Bilqis nodded. "I have taught her. She cooks. Her sister sweeps before going to school and the mother does the washing. I'd be lost without them."

"She used to be a plain little child. I almost did not recognize her."

"She turned twenty last year. It won't be long before her family marries her off."

Kate wanted to ask if she would get to choose her husband, but she resisted the temptation. It was her first trip to Pakistan and everything was foreign. While she had heard Samad talking of servants, and she knew about the babysitters and cleaners who were still familiar and middle-class figures in Australia, or even the butlers and scullery maids of Victorian novels, she had never experienced a life where people did not have to wash clothes, cook meals or clean the house because their servants did everything for them, from the moment they awoke to when they went to bed. Kate glanced at the family as they continued eating, fascinated by this effortless exercise of class superiority.

"I am very cross with you, Shahid," Bilqis said, glancing at Mahbano and then settling her eyes upon her brother-in-law. "If you like my food then why don't you stay with me? I know that you come to Karachi on business, but you never tell me in advance. I only hear about it afterwards. What am I to make of that?"

"I am like a journeyman," said Shahid between mouthfuls. "I don't wish to bother you with my comings and goings."

"There is no bother. Good heavens! I have servants, don't I? Who do I keep all these empty bedrooms for?"

Bilqis could do worse than have him as an ally, and Shahid, who missed nothing, knew what she was thinking. He chuckled with the pleasant air of a man who has everything under control.

Conversation fell into its usual ruts. The men talked, as ever, about politics, bickering about how the country was changing for better or worse. Bilqis and Mahbano exchanged notes on certain common ailments for which their doctors, apparently, had given contradictory prescriptions.

"Get a second opinion," Shahid said to his wife. "Go to Dr. Iqbal and see what he says."

"What if the diagnosis is different again?"

"Then get a third opinion."

"You'd hope that the majority is right," Sikander muttered.

He offered Shahid a cigarette.

"I don't smoke . . ." Shahid started to say, but accepted. He had kicked the habit long ago but the temptation of the occasional nicotine fix was still irresistible, especially if the cigarettes were an imported luxury brand. Blue smoke rose toward the ceiling.

Conversation turned to the referendum of the previous year, when the military dictator had legitimized his martial law in the name of Islam.

"General Zia won't go easily now," Sikander said. "When he overthrew Bhutto he promised to hold elections in ninety days—do you remember? Ninety days. Eight years later, he is still kicking around. That's tenacious, to say the least."

Bilqis told them how she had gone to vote at the polling station at three o'clock in the afternoon. The booths were empty, and the polling staff were busily filling out the forms and stuffing them into the ballot boxes themselves, all with "Yes" votes. "How many forms would you like to fill out?" the polling officer asked her pleasantly as if it were the most normal thing to rig a referendum. She cast a "No" vote and her servants all did the same, but then, she belonged to the heretical minority who had always disliked religious types. When the Electoral Commission result was announced, the General received an incredible 97.7 percent "Yes" vote.

"I did not know that the angels voted too," she said.

"You need not despair," Sikander said. "Most people would have voted 'No' had they understood that they were being asked three questions disguised as one: do you want all laws in conformity with Islam? Do you endorse the Islamization started by General Zia? Do you support the transfer of power to elected representatives of the people? Three separate questions, not linked in my mind; at best, the link is ambiguous. That's what's dishonest about this referendum. It was rigged in favor of a 'Yes' vote by the way the question was framed."

Shahid smiled at him knowingly. "When have elections solved our problems?" he asked, flicking his cigarette ash into an ashtray.

"When have we had free and fair elections?" Bilqis rejoined.

"The only time we had a decent election was in 1970, and the

Bengalis decamped with half of the country. The Pathans and
Baluchis are waiting in line to get their piece next. Keep having
free and fair elections and we won't have anything left."

There was a momentary silence. The atmosphere in the room
changed.

"Democracy does not work for us," Shahid said. "It works in
countries where everyone is educated and secular and thinks alike,
like Britain and Australia. It doesn't work here because we are poor.
Our people are illiterate. They can't even tell their left from right.
What are they going to do with democracy?"

"What's the remedy then? Are we better served by despots?"

"We need to return to the fundamentals," Shahid said. "The
message of Islam has been corrupted over the centuries. There has
not been a pure and just Islamic society since the early days of Islam. We have to bring that back. We don't need alien influences.
All we need to sustain ourselves are the Koran and the Sharia. Until we restore Sharia, we will not regain what is our due."

"What's 'Sharia'?" Kate asked, who was listening with interest.

"It's the Islamic law," Shahid explained.

"What law do you follow now?"

"English law. Our penal code is a legacy of the colonial times."

Sikander dried his neck with a handkerchief and lit another
cigarette, this time without offering one to Shahid. "Fine words,
brother, fine words, but no one has ever explained to me how Sharia will solve our problems. How will it fix corruption? How will it
put food on the table? Will it invoke a fiery jinn to do our bid-
ding?"

Shahid went on eating. "The jinn will be out of the bottle soon,"
he said, "and once it's out, it isn't going back in. Don't tell me then
that I didn't warn you."

Bilqis allowed herself a rueful smile. The litany of national
wounds was at once familiar and true, but inside out, it rang hollow,

narrow-minded, paranoid and self-righteous. Truth had been transformed into a rallying cry by people in quest of power themselves. Bad times, she thought, feeling a certain dimming of strength and authority.

Her face became even darker as she glanced at Samad, her beloved and difficult son. Like most of his wealthy friends, he had gone abroad after high school to study at Western universities and, like them, he delayed his homecoming. His visits became less frequent, which had made it hard for Bilqis to find him a suitable bride. Then, a year ago, he wrote to her saying that he was engaged to Kate.

The letter was remarkably candid. Samad wanted her to understand that he had thought long and hard before making the decision. He loved Kate. He had no intention of breaking the relationship with her, but he wanted his mother's blessings. He was afraid that by marrying a foreign woman he was burning his bridges to his homeland, but he did not want Bilqis to think that he would abandon her to a lonely fate. After these assurances came a passage where he suggested that she ought to move to Australia. He was going to arrange a residence permit for her. Once she had the necessary paperwork, she would always have the option to come and live with him. Of course, she did not have to decide anything just yet, but it was nice to have choices in life. The letter ended on this optimistic note.

Most well-to-do families sent their young men to good universities abroad with the expectation that they would pay attention to their studies. It was also assumed, in an unspoken sort of way, that they might sow their wild oats and do the things that young men must do before settling down. As long as they kept their peccadilloes in the West, no questions were asked. They returned home to sterling careers and arranged marriages and no one was the wiser. There were of course always a few stories of boys marrying foreigners, mostly Germans, for some inexplicable reason, and the occasional English or Scotswoman, but the practice was frowned upon because the fate of mixed marriages was considered grim. The fellows who settled overseas with their foreign wives were never heard of again. Few dared return home to live, afraid that their wives would not adjust in Pakistan and lead unhappy lives.

Tall and thin, with a brooding air, Samad acted as Kate's translator, explaining nuances, and passed her food. He ate little himself and said even less. Bilqis saw him as she always had—a mere boy, who was using exile as an excuse for other failings. An expatriate's envy for the success of friends left behind, a son's guilt for leaving home and the accompanying resentment of thinking that he had not been exonerated from duty—all these fleeting emotions passed over his pale, handsome face as he sat at her table.

Bilqis reached for the fruit platter. There was a tremor in her hands that she tried to conceal. An abyss was opening in her heart. It was not just her son's wedding that made her unhappy. It was a succession of events, all interconnected and related, a pattern of setbacks, rebuffs and hindrances, both within and without, that had formed the fixed idea in her mind that her illustrious family had run out of luck.

2

THE NEXT MORNING, Bilqis awoke early. It had rained before dawn. When it stopped, the frogs started to croak. Bilqis roused from an intense dream, thinking that her husband, Hashmat, was alive. It took her a moment to realize that he had been dead for seven years even though it seemed like yesterday that he was here. Upset with herself, she rose and went into her bathroom. Except for a high vent near the ceiling, it was a small, windowless space, with whitewashed walls and a bouquet of fresh lavender in an alcove. She washed her hands and face with a translucent cake of Pear's soap, dried herself with a thick towel and hung it on a rail. Modern stainless-steel fittings had replaced the original plumbing except for an old cast-iron bathtub that had dug its clawed feet into the floor when the renovators had dared remove it, and threatened to take half of the masonry with it.

She took off her red leather slippers and sat down on the edge of the bathtub. She liked this small bathroom, with its air of a monk's cell. She felt secure here. It was the sanctum sanctorum of her house. She turned on the tap and filled the tub with water. She let the water soak the soles of her feet, sitting on the side of the bathtub until her skin was wrinkled and raw from the cold water. Then she stepped out to look at herself in the mirror. Forty years she had lived in this house. Forty years she had stared into this mirror. For all her marriage and widowhood it had been her home. How could all that time have gone by, passed, as if in a gray blur, as if it carried no weight and was without meaning?

When Hashmat was alive, the couple had moved among the best circles. They led a charmed life, more privileged and fortunate than most. Sometimes she felt afraid because it meant that they had everything to lose. In her own way, she tried to prepare herself for his death. She had been brought up with the idea that men died earlier than women and left them widows picking up the pieces, but she had never imagined the suddenness with which a person could cease to exist.

Hashmat Ali Khan, dead at the age of sixty-two. Heart failure is what the doctor's report said, as if the facts settled the matter, but facts settle nothing at all. Call it heart failure, call it stroke, call it cardiac arrest, call it anything that an autopsy may reveal. The real cause of death is always something else: defeat, grief, loneliness, the accumulation of regret and sorrow that gathers like sediment through a lifetime and one day bursts through. She still found it incomprehensible that a person who woke up, shaved in the mirror and put his clothes on, read the paper, took his medication and went out to the library to return the books, but forgot to return one of them and missed his son's telephone call as well, who became annoyed when he came home and scolded a servant in frustration, grew increasingly glum as the day progressed and so decided to put off calling back his son until his mood improved, did all these things without any undue significance, without knowing that he was doing them for the last time. The consolation was that he had died in her arms. He could have died without preliminaries, in a car crash, or alone in the house, unable to call for help, or he could have died in his sleep, cold, no breath out of his nostrils, while she went on dreaming.

She came down the stairs in her slippers, undid the bolt on the french doors and stepped outside onto the porch. The sea breeze was mercifully fresh, not loaded with the stench of rotting fish that arose as the day drew on. The mornings were still cool even though summer was almost upon them. She braced herself and, dreading a chill, withdrew indoors to put on her cardigan before venturing out again. The garden was hemmed in by a seven-foot-high wall. The pillared gate was cast iron with its original trestlework of monkey tops. A row of neem trees guarded the side facing the road. There were orchids along the other side. A solitary tamarisk grew next to the driveway toward the front. For a moment, she stood still on the porch and breathed calmly and deeply. Then she walked out into the garden and stood in the middle of the lawn. The light was dull gray, softly turning into a bluish hue, and in the lifting gloom she traced the outlines of her home.

The house of limestone block dated from before the Partition. There were three bedrooms upstairs and a fourth one downstairs, which she had turned into her study after her husband's death. The roof was made of red Mangalore tiles. Bougainvillea cascaded down the Roman pillars. A portico led up the main steps onto a veranda with its chessboard floor of black and white tiles. The residence was considered one of the more impressive houses in Old Clifton, this quiet and distinguished seaside suburb. At a distance, it looked magnificent, but like the interior of the house, its external brilliance was deceptive. The cobwebs in the wooden eaves had not been cleaned for years. The rose beds had cracked open in the fierce sun because they hadn't been watered enough. Limp flowers hung from their stems.

Bilqis went to fetch the newspaper lying in the driveway. She noticed a young man standing across the road, watching her with keen eyes. He salaamed her when she met his gaze. Bilqis picked up the newspaper and arose to give him a cursory nod. He came over.

"I am Omar, the new chowkidar," he said. "I look after the property across the road."

"Wasn't there another man who looked after it?"

"He's gone back to his village. He was getting on."

"I didn't know that the owners had hired someone."

"No, they might not have told you," he said, frowning. "I am a seasonal worker. I come here only for the winter months."

"Where are you from?"

"Kashmir."

"That's a long way away."

"I go wherever there is work, begum sahiba. In any event, I thought I'd introduce myself."

"That's good of you," said Bilqis as she started to leave.

"In case you need something, I'll be glad to be of service."

"I don't think that will be necessary," Bilqis said. "My servants take good care of me."

"Of course," he said quickly, "but if there's anything I can do, you know where to find me."

Bilqis gave him a sharp look. His clothes were clean. He had long sideburns and there was stubble on his chin, marking the beginning of a beard. He stood upright with his hands behind his back. He was clearly a lowly employee but there was none of the bowing and salaaming of an obsequious servant about him. His eyes twinkled and laughed as if her status meant nothing to him, and that irreverence troubled her.

When she returned indoors, she found Mahbano sitting in the drawing room with a cup of tea. Like the rest of the house, this room too was sumptuously furnished. Bilqis had ordered the rosewood and cherry sofas from Victoria Furniture on Dundas Road. The old Parsee Curt Virjee was the only craftsman she could find who knew how to make furniture in the French classical style. A sandalwood table inlaid with elephant ivory adorned the center of the room. Against one wall lay a three-piece Louis XVI–style gilded set comprising a settee and two armchairs. On the opposite side lay a musty rolled-arm sofa covered in green moquette. Two wing chairs, with their backs toward the french doors, faced inward. Bilqis had put them there to hide the marks of rising damp on the walls where the paint was beginning to peel. A beautiful old piano with ivory keys stood against the wall in a corner. It had been out of tune for years.

Bilqis closed the french doors and came to sit next to her sister. Mumtaz entered with the trolley, bringing a fresh pot of tea, and placed it beside the two women. Mahbano glanced at the tea service after the girl left. The cups were neatly arranged in saucers with spoons. The pot was set under a cozy imprinted with cats, with a small pitcher of milk and a tea strainer beside it. Everything was perfectly laid out.

"You've trained her well," Mahbano said. "Who will do the work when she's gone?"

"The younger sister, of course," Bilqis replied, smiling. "I have her in reserve but she has much to learn and I doubt that she'll ever be as good."

"Count your blessings, for I still don't have a servant."

"You always lose them," Bilqis said flatly. "I've told you why—you're a tyrant. You push them too far."

Bilqis poured the tea and refilled her sister's cup. They sat for a little while without exchanging a word. Mahbano was waiting for Bilqis to say something about her trip. Bilqis had flown to Melbourne to meet Kate and her family and to attend the wedding there. She had returned a few weeks ago to make preparations for the Pakistani reception.

"Have you unpacked?" Mahbano asked.

Bilqis shook her head. "My suitcases are still lying under my bed. The other night I dreamed that the bedroom had turned upside down. The fan was on the floor and the bed was on the ceiling. Even the cockroaches were walking upside down."

"Your dreams are turning topsy-turvy," Mahbano said. "It's a sign that you've come back from Down Under. What did you think of it?"

Bilqis allowed herself a faint smile. "It's a strange place, I have to say. Very remote and isolated. It's hard to imagine that places like that still exist in this day and age, but amazingly, they do. If you read their newspapers, you'd think that Australia was all there was to the world. The rest of it might as well fall off the map. You'd have to go there to know what I mean."

"Did you do any sightseeing?"

"A lot," Bilqis said approvingly. "It's a big country and the distances are very large. They think nothing of driving a few hundred miles a day, but whoever went on naming the places probably had another landscape in mind. What they call a mountain is a mound for us. What they call alpine country are our hillocks, hot and arid and full of flies. Their rivers are like our streams. Everything is called Great this, Great that but it's not as great or grand as it sounds, except for the outback, which is apparently something else."

"I liked the postcards you sent."

"Melbourne is pretty," Bilqis said. "It has its theaters and museums, but it feels empty compared to Karachi. There were so few people about that I thought that an epidemic had wiped out the population. The neighborhoods are quieter than our cemeteries. Sometimes I felt that the whole city was on the verge of becoming a ghost town. It takes a while to get used to it."

"You met the girl's parents, of course?"

"Yes."

"So what happened?"

"I don't think that Samad had prepared them for what to expect.

They thought that I would be some dumb, veiled woman—some sort of coolie's wife."

Mahbano laughed. "What were you wearing?"

"I was wearing what I always wear: my white sari and my pearls. I ought to have worn my pants. Then I spoke—I think they were quite shocked to hear English coming out of my mouth. They're not the most well-traveled people. They've never been outside Australia."

"I suppose they won't be coming to the reception, then."

Bilqis gave her a cool glance.

"Oh come, you had little time to know them," Mahbano protested.

"Little time or a lot of time—it makes no difference," Bilqis said, arching her eyebrows. "They are not like us. They don't understand us or our values, and, to be quite honest, they are people of whom we know nothing."

"They could say the same things about us."

"Don't be so sure. I didn't see a single book in their house."

"But they are decent people?"

"Well, they are courteous and civil, and hospitable enough, but there was an edge to their manners, a forced friendliness that seemed to me like a reproach."

"That's natural, isn't it? They were probably just as nervous as you were."

Bilqis ignored the remark.

"Tell me more about the girl," Mahbano said.

"She's a lawyer."

"Oh really?" Mahbano was impressed. "Does she wear a wig and appear in court?"

"No, she is a solicitor, not a barrister," Bilqis said. It annoyed her that Mahbano did not know the difference. Her sister, for all her pretensions, often showed herself to be a complete ignoramus. What did education have to do with all this anyway? It was about self-preservation. A family's lineage survived through the continuity of its traditions. Kate could be the most educated woman in the world, but would she teach her children the prayers, the rituals, the feast days and the fast days? Who would the children marry when they grew up? What faith would they have? Traditions and etiquette that had flourished for generations would come to an end with her. It was akin to slow and gradual extinction.

Mahbano could see that Bilqis was disappointed. She had considered her son worthy of princesses, and he had gone and married a middle-class white girl from Melbourne. Considerations about form and prestige that worried Bilqis made Mahbano uneasy as well, but being who she was and knowing what she knew, she wondered if her sister was feeling wronged because her will had not been done.

"I am sure that he did not set out to go against my wishes," Bilqis said, "but there he was, all alone, and a nice-looking woman came along and wooed him. What was he supposed to do?"

"Are you sure that it was she who wooed him? Maybe he wooed her."

"Whatever he did, he probably wasn't thinking. He is young and bound to make mistakes when there is no one to guide him. I had a good mind to summon him back and keep him here until he forgot about her. I would have found him a pretty, well-groomed girl from society right here."

"You can't force his will."

"I know," Bilqis said without looking up. "He is headstrong like you."

"She has converted, hasn't she?" Mahbano asked.

Bilqis winced at the question, because conversion was only partial redemption. It conferred the religion but it never made one equal.

"Yes, but tell me, is it natural for two people from different cultures, races and backgrounds, who have grown up in completely different surroundings, to share a destiny together? Can such a union ever be a happy one? What if she leaves him one day? Isn't that what these women do?"

"You know what my views are."

"You think it's wise to marry someone you love, don't you?"

"What's the alternative?"

"I didn't love Hashmat when we got married, but I grew to love him and respect him all the same. It came with time. Our parents didn't love each other when they got married. They didn't even know each other before their wedding night, but that didn't stop them from living a long life together."

"You did what you could," Mahbano said. "Now give him your blessing and leave the rest to fate. It's a blessing if our children are happy. God willing, everything else will turn out all right."

"Yes, sister, yes . . ." Bilqis sighed. "In a perfect world, everything should turn out all right, but we live in an imperfect world, where nobility must follow a moral code and behave in a manner that is incorruptible. Make no mistake. People measure us against this ideal. They wait for us to fall below a certain level and, when some unfortunate soul happens to slip, their judgment is swift."

3

WHILE KATE WAS getting ready to go downstairs for breakfast, Hameeda entered her room to take the washing away. Kate greeted her and then watched her from the corner of her eye as the old woman sat on the floor and separated the colored fabrics from the rest. Hameeda's hair was completely white. Her face was deeply lined and her skin was leathery, like parchment left to dry in the sun. A creature from a medieval bestiary, Kate thought. After Hameeda had gone and Mumtaz came to clean the room, Kate could not help thinking that, one day, the girl might look like her mother too. Neither chance nor coincidence could alter that face. It would become what it had to become, predestined like her fate.

The girl lived in cramped quarters at the back of the house with her parents, younger sister and two older brothers. The eldest, who was married, lived with his young wife and son under the same roof. Kate saw no seclusion or privacy in the arrangement. It seemed a hard life. And was that not also the mystery: that servants could keep on serving their masters without question and their children would do the same? All her life, Kate had lived with people who were like her. To see people who were clearly of a lower order aroused in her feelings of compassion. Mumtaz struck her as obedient but remote and obscure. What were her thoughts? What did she feel? She understood no English apart from a few basic words, which sufficed with gestures for basic communication, but since the two young women were alone now, Kate decided to attempt a conversation.

"Wedding," she said, pointing to the dress that she was going to wear at the reception. It was spread out on the bed, waiting to be ironed. Items of clothing, boxes full of bangles, jewelry and shoes lay scattered everywhere. Mumtaz looked at her, smiled and continued dusting.

"You wedding?" Kate tried again.

Mumtaz shook her head.

"Love?"

Mumtaz blushed. She knew the word, of course, but what was the meaning of these questions? What business did the memsahib have probing into her life? She felt embarrassed at being cornered like this, but then she looked at the kindly eyes and sensed sincerity. Kate was beautiful, she thought. Beauty elevated a person. It overcame obstacles. If only she could be like her, she'd be the happiest person in the world, but their destinies could not have been further apart. Of course, she knew all about Kate. This was the girl who had stolen Samad from his mother. This was the girl who had caused so much heartache. It was so easy to dislike her, except that she obviously did not know the harm she had created. Kate was innocent, like a rose, Mumtaz thought, innocent and lovely, except for the thorns in her sides.

Later in the morning, Bilqis went looking for Kate and found her in the study. She was sitting on a pink armless couch in a corner, thumbing through a thick reference book. She rose to greet Bilqis.

"Do sit down," Bilqis said mildly. "Have you been reading? I won't bother you then. I'll just open the windows to let in some air. It gets so stuffy here sometimes."

"You're not bothering me at all," Kate answered. "I was just marveling at your collection of books. It's impressive. Are they all yours?"

"Some of them belonged to my father's library and some belonged to Hashmat, my husband, but I suppose they are all mine now."

The room was furnished simply, although the ornate style of the carpenter who had decorated the rest of the house was also apparent here. Bookcases in heavy dark wood lined the walls. Popular hardbacks by Alistair MacLean, James A. Michener and M. M. Kaye were packed alongside Proust, Mann, Balzac and Melville. Another cabinet was crammed with an Urdu collection of poetry anthologies by Mir, Sauda, Ghalib and Faiz.

Bilqis looked at the book in Kate's hand. "I remember studying the Funk and Wagnalls dictionary when I was a child," she said, as she sat down at her desk. "If my memory serves me right, it has been prepared by more than three hundred and eighty specialists and features twelve representative types of swine. My head is full of such trivia. It had once belonged to my father's library in Calcutta, you see. There were seven thousand books behind the glass cases of his shelves, each carrying his private stamp on the inside cover. A stuffed Bengal tiger watched over them. I went there because I felt safe. I loved the texture of his books. I liked to hold them in my hands and feel their weight. They were my friends. I could recognize each one by its own smell. The first book I read was about Aladdin and his magic lamp. My mother bought it for me. I thought I had to memorize it. For a long time, I couldn't get the idea out of my mind, of memorizing storybooks, I mean. It took me a while to get used to reading for pleasure. It seemed so decadent at first, to read a book and forget it, but once I got used to it I couldn't get enough of books."

"Were you born in Calcutta?"

"I grew up there but I was born in Darjeeling, in the Indian Himalayas."

"I've heard it's a beautiful place."

"It used to be," Bilqis mused. "I used to go there when I was young, in the twenties. My parents owned a gabled chalet, where we spent our summers. I remember little ponies cantering about the streets. Sometimes the clouds came so low that you could not see the mountains for days, but when you saw them, it was like a vision."

"I'd love to go one day."

"I wouldn't go myself. I suspect it's a bit of a relic now."

"Did your parents come to Pakistan too?" Kate asked.

"My father did. He had done well for himself in India. He used to be in the army but he was retired and he came for our sake. My mother passed away shortly before we decided to move. I don't think she would have liked to be buried anywhere else. She loved India too much."

"It must have been hard for you."

"Well, it's never hard for young people. It's only hard for old people. Our servants cried when we bade them farewell. They had served us all their lives. I had grown up in their arms but I remember feeling more happy than sad when I left them. It was my great adventure. My father, who had never shed a tear in his life, shook like a tree."

"Have you been back?"

"No, it's not easy for us to go back anymore. I suppose it never was. The politics have made it nearly impossible now. I don't like that, I must admit. When we left India, we imagined that we'd be able to come and go freely once things settled down. While we were horrified by the riots and massacres, we parted with our cousins and aunts and uncles, giving assurances to one another that the two countries would come to terms and normal traffic would resume as if there were no borders because, no matter what the politicians said, the people were still the same on both sides, cut from the same cloth. I never saw them again. Being banished from a place is different from leaving by choice. In any event, I shouldn't complain. We've done well for ourselves here. We wouldn't have had this life in India."

Kate changed the subject. "Do you read a lot now?"

"I do, mostly authors who have long since died. I am sure that there are a great many authors writing some very good books these days, but there comes a time when you stop following the fashions because you've had your fill. I stopped about thirty years ago. You'll have to go back to the fifties and early sixties if you want to know what I like. It's the same with films and music, I am afraid. I only listen to what you might call old-fashioned music and watch old-fashioned films, as I am set in my ways. Pop music is too loud and jarring for my taste, and, well, the less said about modern cinema, the better. I think that everything was more brilliant and wonderful in my youth than it is now. The world was more innocent. Literature was pure. Music was good. I can go on, but I won't bore you because I know I am wrong. Not everyone is like that, of course. My husband kept up his interests until he passed on. What did you read as a child?"

"Enid Blyton, among others," Kate said, "but Blyton was my favorite."

"I should have known," Bilqis remarked, pleased. "Blyton is the patron saint of the colonies. You won't find an Indian child who is not familiar with Enid Blyton. We don't like to admit it, but she brought England into our hearts. Samad read her too. We still have his collection somewhere in the house. Nothing gets thrown away here, you see. What else did you read?"

"I read the Blinky Bill books and Snugglepot and Cuddlepie. They are books about the Australian bush. I don't suppose you know them. I loved them because my grandparents had a farm."

"I am not familiar with them," replied Bilqis. "I started reading *The Tree of Man* by Patrick White on the plane from Australia but I haven't finished yet. Have you read him?"

"No, I haven't. I mean to, though. These days I don't find much time after work. I often have to work late and, by the time I've finished dinner, it's time for bed. I used to read a lot at university."

Bilqis went to her bookshelf and shelved a couple of books that were lying loose on top of the others. Across the hallway, she heard the clatter of plates and cups in the kitchen.

"One day I'd like to teach my students something about Australian writing."

"Samad told me about your work. Have you always lectured in literature?"

"Only since my husband died," Bilqis said. "I give occasional lectures and I do so mainly for my own amusement. The chancellor is a family friend and he obliges me."

"Perhaps I could come to your classes too."

"You'd have to be here though. Have you thought about living here?"

"Not really," Kate said. "Would you like us to?"

"What mother doesn't want her child to be near?"

Kate thought of her own mother.

"In our culture," Bilqis said, "a wife follows in her husband's footsteps. She goes where he goes. She leaves her family to become part of his family. That's what I did and my mother and my grandmother and my great-grandmother before me. It's the way we are."

Kate felt put out. Samad had come to live in her country before he had even met her. She did not see why, by marrying him, she was obliged to live in his country. Had she not converted to Islam for his sake? Didn't she have to explain herself to her friends and acquaintances? Wasn't that enough?

"Why of course, we'll try to, but it would be hard for me to come and live in a country that's so different from my own. For a start, I don't even know the language."

"You'd learn it."

"I wouldn't be able to work."

"That can be arranged."

"But women aren't supposed to work here. They're meant to stay at home."

"You are my daughter-in-law," Bilqis replied. "If you want to work, you shall find it. I shall make it so. I go to work, don't I?"

"I suppose so."

"But if you had the choice between work and family, what would you choose?"

Kate laughed. "I know what I have to say to please you."

"I don't want you to please me. I want you to tell me what you think."

"Then I'd say that the choice is not so black and white."

"You'd like to work. I can tell."

"Work is important to me, but I don't have ambitions. I don't want to become a partner in a law firm or anything of that sort. I'm quite happy to choose family but I'd like to keep a connection to my work. I wouldn't like to give up that aspect of myself completely."

"If you lived here, you'd be able to work because you'd have servants. You'd have the best of both worlds."

Kate reflected. "Perhaps," she said. "We could come and visit you as often as you liked."

"Like tourists?" Bilqis smiled.

Kate drew herself together and looked at Bilqis quizzically. "You could come and visit us," she said.

"Travel is starting to take its toll on me. At my age, if one goes away on a journey, one never knows if one might ever return."

"You could come and live in Australia."

Bilqis fixed her with a stare. "Did my son put that idea in your head?"

When Kate said nothing, Bilqis lowered her eyes. She examined her fingers and spoke in a good-humored tone. "I know. He thinks he owes me a duty. It's as if everyone will live happily ever after if I migrated."

"Of course you should think about it," Kate said quickly. "Life would be easier in Melbourne."

"For you or for me?" Bilqis chuckled. "If it's hard for you to come and live here, then imagine how hard it would be for me to go and live over there. You are still young. I am old. I am not going to learn any new tricks."

"But if something happened, who would you turn to?"

"Why, I have my servants."

As if on cue, Mumtaz came in with two cups of tea. The women stopped talking while Bilqis gave her instructions. Kate noticed that Mumtaz did not meet her eyes while she listened to her mistress. She did not mind because she understood that the veiled gaze was a form of acknowledgment itself. The bond between Bilqis and Mumtaz seemed stronger to her than her own link with Bilqis. Despite apparent differences, there was no distance between Bilqis and the girl. They were one and the same. She was the outsider. So much was plain.

"I'd like to give her something," Kate said to Bilqis after Mumtaz was gone. "She has been very good to me and I'd like to show her my appreciation."

"What do you have in mind?"

"Oh, a nice hair clip or a silver bracelet. What do you think?"

Bilqis laughed. "I wouldn't suggest a hair clip. She braids her hair. She would never wear a clip, although I am sure that she would keep it. Give her a hundred rupees. That's what I would suggest."

"I can afford more than a hundred," Kate said.

"It's up to you. Give her a bracelet if you want, but if you give her silver this time then she'd expect gold next time. You'd be setting a precedent."

"But if I give her something less, won't she know that I can afford more? She has seen my dowry and the things that you have given me."

"The dowry I have given you is not going to be a lot more than what I will give her when she gets married," Bilqis said, not without a certain amount of satisfaction. "You have to realize that she is not an ordinary employee. Her family has been here since I have been here and they're going to be here for as I long as I live. I may not shower them with money but I am responsible for their well-being. When Hameeda's grandson fell ill with jaundice, I paid for his hospital. When her husband got himself into debt, I paid it off. They serve me and that's all well and good. I expect them to be honest and faithful to me, but my obligations to them are absolute."

Kate picked up her teacup and walked around the room, looking at a cluster of framed photographs on one of the bookcases. It seemed to her that she had failed some test, but she drew herself together. She was here now and she could do nothing but let the conversation play itself out.

"There's my husband," Bilqis said, pointing to a picture of a young man smoking a pipe. "It's from his Oxford days. And that man, posing with the dead tiger at his feet, is my grandfather. And that's a picture of Sikander and me with my parents, standing on the lawn of our home in Calcutta. I am about ten years old there."

"Who's the child in your arms?" Kate asked.

"Mahbano," Bilqis said.

"She looks tiny," Kate said.

"Yes, you wouldn't think that she was that small once."

Bilqis began to tell Kate of her lineage and how time and circumstance had sapped the family of its titles and land. One of her most vivid memories was attending the silver-jubilee celebrations of King George V in Comilla, where she sat under an immense white marquee and watched a parade of elephants go trumpeting past, bedecked in saffron robes and jewels. She was sixteen or seventeen years old.

"You know, my family used to have fabulous wealth before 1857. On my mother's side, we were related to the royal family of Oudh. Palaces, palanquins, paradise gardens and peacocks—we had it all," Bilqis said. "My great-great-grandfather was the maternal uncle of the king of Oudh and one of the richest men of Deccan. There's a story that, for fourteen years, he stubbornly refused to accept defeat in a kite-flying match. Every time his kite was brought down by his adversary, he had a new one sent up. For fourteen long years, he and his servants flew the kites, day and night, sunshine or rain. One of his nieces fought the British during the Mutiny. She surrounded the British in the Lucknow Residency and kept them there until reinforcements arrived from outside. She retreated when her forces were defeated, but she never surrendered. Even when Queen Victoria issued a general amnesty to all rebels, she turned it down and demanded that India be restored to the Indians.

"Our fortunes have been in decline for nearly a century, ever since the Mutiny, in fact, when the British annexed our lands. What estates they spared were divided and subdivided by the family as its numbers grew. My parents could no longer afford the lifestyle that my grandparents could, and their circumstances, in turn, were more circumscribed than those of their parents. The

Partition only hastened the fall. We are people of empire. The decline and fall of our fortunes is also the decline and fall of our people. We think of our past when we imagine our future and we have nothing to console us but myths of a golden age.

"Are there any other people who do not differentiate between past and future? Only we have the same word for tomorrow as for yesterday. Time is not our enemy. We are not afraid of clocks. If you spend a year among us, you will know what I mean. We never do things in a hurry. We are an indolent people; no, that is not quite correct—our lack of individuality gives us certain liberties. We are a communal people. We don't differentiate between private and public spheres. We like the comfort of others. That's why we need our servants and they, let's not forget, need us. We are passive, yes, we tend towards repose but it is a state of mind which we, the old families at least, develop to cocoon ourselves from the corruption around us.

"I suppose what I am telling you is that Samad comes from an old family. We are known to everyone here. Even strangers have heard of us. I can tell people who I am and, if they don't know me personally, they will know immediately that I am someone to be reckoned with. That's the way we are. We are aristocracy in name only but antiquity still carries some weight in these regions. Names and titles evoke magical powers. What I am saying is that Samad need not have left this country."

Kate had known that the challenge was coming and now it was here. So this was how it was going to happen, she thought. This was how her mother-in-law was going to broach the issues, because these were the only things that mattered for her.

"Why, of course, Mrs. Khan," she remarked. "You are a brave mother to have let him go."

"And you are an intelligent girl," Bilqis said. "You love my son?"

"We love each other."

Bilqis smiled reproachfully. Love, she thought, those hackneyed words, that dross garnered from films and novels. And a marriage that was built on love and love alone, and the premise that love would be the remedy against all odds, was that not naïve and narrow-minded and self-regarding, at the expense of everything else?

"Is he the first man you have loved?"

Kate bristled, understanding perfectly what was meant. "I don't think that you have to love just one person in your life," she said.

"I did."

"Did you have a choice?"

Bilqis did not reply. Her worries, her love for Samad and her confusion on his behalf blurred everything.

"I don't think there's only one way to love," Kate continued. "You can fall in love when you are too young or with the wrong person, or the right person for the wrong reason, but you wouldn't want to marry someone without love. I married Samad because of a whole lot of coincidences. We could so easily have not met. I could so easily have loved someone else, but not in the same way that I love Samad."

Here was a girl who spoke her mind, Bilqis thought, but instead of feeling angry or upset with her, she found herself pitying her. Kate seemed so keen to prove herself, so eager to win her trust, and yet Bilqis had a persistent feeling that no matter how long she interrogated her daughter-in-law, and how many questions she asked her, she would never get to the bottom of her.

4

IT WAS THE evening before the reception. The young couple were alone in the guest room, formerly Samad's bedroom. The windows were open and Kate was sitting up on the bed reading a book. Samad was lying on his back, staring at the ceiling fan as it spun around. For the first time in weeks, he was able to take a step back and consider where he had arrived in his life. When he first met Kate, he thought it would be just a quick fling. He didn't think that he would ever fall in love with her, and here he was, married to her. The sleepy look in her hazel eyes, the rose-pink nail polish on the tips of her fingers, the warmth of her skin, still aroused in him the same desire that he had felt for her at the beginning, but he could not help wondering whether he had done the right thing. With perfect foresight, would he have married her?

As the reception drew nearer, he sensed her nervousness increase. He could well imagine how out at sea she felt about what was expected of her. At first, the transformation she was required to undergo had seemed like an amusing masquerade, but its serious nature soon became apparent. The previous night, before the family dinner, there was a simple ceremony where the two of them became man and wife under Islamic law.

Kate blanched when the mullah asked her if she had become a Muslim. She knew very well that saying yes was a mere legal formality, but what if the mullah had demanded tangible proof, asking her to recite a verse, tell the sequence of a prayer? The whole world would know that she had undergone only a facile conversion. She was even more dismayed when Samad told her that his mother had obliged the mullah in advance with a thick envelope filled with cash. So it was not a miracle that he had remained docile. Now she understood that no matter how well she passed muster with her in-laws and their friends, acceptance was another matter altogether. This knowledge weighed on Samad too. He found the atmosphere in the house oppressive. The slow process of decay seemed accelerated when he returned home after long absences. One year, his mother's hair had wisps of gray, two years later, it had turned white; other details that he had never noticed before now revealed themselves to him—the yellowed books, the tarnished silver picture frames and the mildewed sofas with their worn edges—like possessions in a burial chamber, all balms, unguents and mummies, all destined to years of oblivion at the back of a scrap dealer's shop. These impressions lashed at him like strikes of a flail, undermining every achievement of his life by suggesting the cost of his material success. Each time he returned home, the visit brought into relief his responsibility of caring for his mother. There was no immediate urgency, of course, to care for her, but was it not a matter of time before her need of him would become obvious? A person must be absolved of guilt to savor success. Coming back only magnified his guilt because it questioned his rationale for leaving home in the first place. How could he redeem himself when, by marrying a foreigner, he was repudiating the possibility of ever coming home? Even if he was somehow absolved of guilt, how could he justify the meaning of living among people not his own, speaking a language not his own?

Despite these thoughts, he tried to remain calm and unruffled. He did not wish to alarm Kate, or let his mother glimpse his insecurities, because that would vindicate her doubts. Instead, he tried to spend as much time away from home as possible. He took Kate on outings and showed her all the sights. Karachi was never a beautiful city. It was a dusty port town that had mushroomed since the Partition without any outline or any general aesthetic sense, so that even the old parts seemed closed in and stifled by the swelling multitudes. The daytime sun was mean, the bazaars were seething and most of the fine old buildings were derelict. But despite the neglected, dilapidated sights, the appalling traffic and the bystanders who seemed to appear everywhere like idle legions, Kate enjoyed these excursions. She liked it when old shopkeepers recognized Samad and referred to her as their "memsahib," but Samad, in his guilt, interpreted these remarks as being for his benefit—by marrying a "memsahib," he had broken ranks with his people. He felt ashamed of himself for taking her on these expeditions. He felt that he had two selves inside. Kate belonged to his new self, but the places of his past belonged to his old self, and the two contradicted and violated each other's spheres.

To escape this inner turmoil, he drove her to the wharf at Boat Basin one day and hired a motorboat that took them out onto the bay. There they told the skipper to cut the motor and let the boat drift while they ate freshly cooked crabmeat and sipped cold drinks. Only when he found himself alone with Kate, far from everyone and everything that was familiar to him, did Samad's insecurities evaporate. He experienced a sense of elevation then, of ascending from confusion to a rarified plane, where he could see the true order of things. What did it matter if he had become distanced from his own people? He was close to the woman he loved. He did not need anyone else. When they came ashore, he was at peace again.

He was remembering that feeling as he lay on his bed. Kate looked up from her book. "Your mother spoke to me," she said.

"Did she? I suppose it was about time that you two had a chat."

"Yes, we talked a great deal. She likes to talk."

"Well, she doesn't talk to me."

"Maybe you don't let her."

"What did she say?"

"We talked about books and what we liked to read. She told me about herself and where she grew up. All sorts of things."

"I am glad."

"Can I ask you something?"

"Sure."

"Do you think you should marry the person you love?"

"Yes, of course. What sort of question is that?"

"Your mother thinks that love isn't enough."

"What's enough?"

"You have to offer something more than love, utter submission or total devotion. I don't know."

"I think the word you are looking for is selflessness."

"A wife's selflessness?"

"Towards her husband, yes."

"What about the husband's selflessness?"

"I am just telling you how my mother thinks. For a good wife, the husband always comes first."

"Sometimes I wonder if you have the same notions."

"I wouldn't have married you if I had those notions."

"You don't expect us to live here, do you?" she asked.

"I don't expect it."

"But would you prefer that we did?"

"I've never asked you to, and frankly . . ."

"Yes?"

"Frankly, I don't want you to make sacrifices for me."

"I've converted for you, haven't I?"

"Yes, but what's the big deal? You're the same person as before, aren't you?"

"No, I'm not. I feel different."

"How can you feel different? You haven't changed. You haven't started praying or fasting or worshipping a different God."

"Would you have converted for me?"

"Preferably not," Samad said, grinning. "In Islam, the penalties are too harsh."

Kate looked at him intently. "Your mother would like us to live here. Would you come back if she asked you to?"

"My mother would like many things. She has her hopes," he said. "I don't have to do everything she asks."

"Would you have come back had you married a local girl?"

"You realize that that is a loaded question?"

"I'd like to know."

"Well, if you must know, then perhaps. It is the difference between knowing what you can or can no longer do. I might not have made the choice of coming back, but the option would have been there."

"And now you find yourself trapped?"

Samad chuckled. "You ask too many questions," he said.

"I just want to know what you are thinking."

Samad's face darkened. He knew that once she began, Kate had the judicial habit of pursuing a line of questioning until she had arrived at a conclusion. It was futile to stop now. It was so often like this between them, light banter became serious at the turn of a phrase. All too easily was a gesture misunderstood, a nuance misplaced, and, in a moment, the exchange brought up some deep and buried resentment, like a sunny day becoming overcast without warning.

The truth was that Samad did not want to return. He felt

indifferent about Pakistan, for most of the time anyway, although it hadn't always been like this. His attachment had weakened to a point where he couldn't care less about it. Sometimes he even despised the place. It was only the idea of return that appealed to him, the possibility of coming back to where he had grown up, and the spiritual solace of knowing that the door was not shut on him. How could he ever explain these things to Kate? She did not have to struggle with a lost past. She did not have to contend with home, birthplace and identity. She did not know what it meant to reconcile these things with her own time and place. How could she understand him?

He got up to draw the curtains. "I married you because I love you," he said. "I wouldn't have done it if I thought I'd be trapped."

"But your mother is a consideration, isn't she?"

"Of course she is."

"Do you know how she feels about us?"

"Oh, I can make a good guess."

Samad came back to the bed. He spoke the words with such hostility that Kate had to smile, relieved that she alone was not the cause of his distress. The anxiety melted from her features.

"I don't want you to be unhappy."

"I am not."

"But if your mother is unhappy, then you must be unhappy too."

"Why should I feel accountable for how she feels?"

"You do. It's obvious."

"Well, we hardly talk, so I can't be reading her mind."

"Do you think she understands you?"

"I think her idea of who I am is fifteen years out of date."

"Maybe you should talk to her more."

"That's not possible."

"Why not?"

"We've been far away from each other for too long."

"That's a pathetic excuse."

"Time and distance change everything."

"How?"

"The longer you stay away, the less you see of each other, the less you have to say to each other. It's the little things that matter, but how can you talk about them when you lead separate lives? You can't share them with someone thousands of miles away without reducing and diminishing them. Imagine talking to your mother on the telephone month after month, year after year, without ever seeing her. I wager you'll run out of things to say."

"But you can talk to her when you come home and when she visits us."

"It's not like you throw a switch and everything returns to normality," Samad said. "If you are not part of another person's life, then what you don't share with each other is lost. You can't make up for it. You can't record anecdotes and replay them again. You can't store up conversations. Well, you can, of course, but you can't recount things in the same spirit once their moment has passed. It's like going through someone else's photo album. It's not the same as being there."

"Well, if you can't talk to her, then hug her, at least," Kate said, reaching out to him. "Show her some compassion. It's really not that hard."

Samad was pleased because he thought that she was feeling responsible for his mother. It gave him satisfaction to know that it was not just he who suffered. He let her fingers touch his hand, but he withdrew it after a moment. There was someone at the door. Mumtaz had come to paint henna on Kate's hands.

5

SAMAD WAS A banker. A graduate of Oxford and Yale, he worked for a string of management consultants before joining an investment bank in New York. By the time he was in his late twenties, he was regarded as one of the bank's brightest executives. After postings in London and Hong Kong, he was sent to Melbourne, where the bank had opened a new office. He took a flat in St. Kilda, close to the beach, and furnished it with basic but well-made furniture. He worked hard. He had a few affairs but none of them were serious. In his spare time, he read books and went to see films. He did not mind being alone—he liked his freedom. A good deal of the money he earned he sent to Bilqis, despite her protests. The rest he spent on himself. He was a reserved man and did not make friends easily, but he had great concern for the friends he had. He thought nothing of flying halfway around the world to see them.

In his second year, he met Kate. The bank had recently closed a multibillion-dollar transaction and the bank's law firm had arranged an evening of champagne and canapés in an art gallery to celebrate the closing. It was the usual turnout of bankers, businessmen and lawyers, milling around paintings and chatting with one another in voices that grew louder as the champagne flowed. Kate stood apart from the crowd, sipping a martini with another girl. She worked at the bank's law firm but Samad had not met her before. He thought that she was the most attractive woman there. Her manner was serious and she had a certain reserve, but she listened to him with interest when he introduced himself. He was flattered by her attention and found himself immediately drawn to her.

The following week, they went out for dinner. They ordered pasta in a small, crowded Italian restaurant in Carlton. From the window, they could see young men of Italian descent cruising by in their souped-up cars. They joked about them, ate slowly and stayed at the table till late, having one of those conversations that is hardly memorable in itself but leaves behind a heady, exhilarating feeling that one never forgets. The next week they met on Chapel Street for a meal and walked to the Astor afterward to see *Doctor Zhivago*. The tram tracks glistened in the aftermath of a light summer shower. The Astor was an artifact from another time, an Art Deco temple. Samad liked its sweeping staircases and marble balustrades, with their aerodynamic lines. It was a utopian building but at the same time it seemed apocalyptic, doomed, as if the future that it represented also contained within it the past. The association of ideas aroused in him the fatalism that he felt about his life sometimes. It was the feeling that no matter what he accomplished, he could not change his fundamental nature. He saw the world from a different perspective than did a European or an American. The more he assimilated and the more perspectives he developed, the more divided he felt, wanting to be in one place and being in another, and then being in that place and wanting to return, as if he had two souls, two consciences and two wills. This inner division, he feared, would be his undoing.

The film finished very late, and, as there weren't any taxis, Samad walked Kate back to her place. It was a pleasant evening. Even close to midnight, the air was warm. A slight breeze rustled through the trees. In the dim light of streetlamps, they walked close together, brushing each other's hands. Kate wore a long flowing skirt that she told him had belonged to her grandmother. Her hair was tied up, with wisps of it loose around her face and neck. It was pleasant listening to her talk about her family, descendants of French Huguenots. Her grandparents sold wool, and their forebears grew barley and wheat. On her father's side, her great-great-grandfather was a judge of sheepdog trials. He had six daughters and four sons to feed, and they lived in a two-room house with a tin roof. In twenty years, he never missed a show but his farm suffered the usual setbacks of droughts and floods. During the depression years of the 1890s, he went prospecting for gold at Ballarat, fell down an old mine shaft and died. Her mother's ancestors had to live in tents when they got off the boat from Liverpool. One of them was a carpenter and opened the first coffin shop in Melbourne. They were hard up too.

They started talking about their grandfathers, who had both fought in the First World War. Samad's grandfather saw action at the Somme with the Indian army. Kate's grandfather fought with the Anzacs at Verdun. They both survived the war.

"What was he like, your grandfather?" Samad asked.

"He was a mean person."

"Was he mean to you?"

"He was mean to everyone except me!"

"Was it the war that changed him?"

"No, he was always mean, a drunk and a bully, apparently. He was like that when he left and he was the same when he came back. Not everyone who fought in the war was noble."

"My grandfather was suffering from dementia when he died," Samad said. "I was seven years old. He did not know me. I had to be introduced to him each time we saw each other, even though he lived in the same house as us. He did not even know his children anymore. My own mother was a stranger to him. 'Where's that woman who was here a while ago?' he used to ask if she went out of sight. He did not know that she was his own daughter. My mother cried a lot when he died, but I think she was relieved. It was a weight off her shoulders."

"Old age can be a terrible thing," Kate said.

"Yes, especially if you are alone."

"My grandmother was alone. She left my grandfather when we were growing up. My mother said that she could not put up with him any longer."

"It must have affected your mother."

"No, she was happy for her, actually. Grandmother was a changed person after she left him. She came out of her shell. She joined a bowling club. She started to paint. I never knew that she could paint so well. She used to do wonderful gum trees and dry-creek landscapes. We still have some of them in my parents' house."

"And what happened to him?"

"Oh, he went into a nursing home. One morning they found him dead. He'd passed away in his sleep. His medals were next to his pillow, arranged in a neat line. He used to tinker with them to put himself to sleep, like a child.

"It's sad," Kate added after a pause. "Everyone used to say that he was a bastard, but he was always kind to me. He used to watch me play for hours. No one else had so much time for me."

They walked in silence, lost in thought. Kate lived in a flat on a quiet side lane off Chapel Street, on the other side of the busy Dandenong Road. They passed a row of Victorian terraced houses.

"Would you like to come in?" she asked as they came to her door.

"For a little while," Samad said.

"You don't have to be shy," she said, laughing. "I'm harmless."

The street was empty. In the night sky, the moon shone bright. Kate unlocked the door and they went in. In the hallway, Samad saw an old photograph of her great-grandparents hanging in a frame. He looked at their faces, their eyes, the woman's thin lips, the man's large, powerful hands, and imagined them to be tough, resilient people. Kate poured some wine while he rummaged through her music collection.

"I didn't think that women liked rock music," Samad said.

"What did you think I liked?"

"Debussy or Satie, something classy."

"What if I said that I liked Barry Manilow?"

"I'd walk."

"Would you?"

"No, I like Elton John, so we're in the same boat."

"I don't think so," she said, laughing. "I don't like Barry Manilow at all. I was only joking."

"Okay. Is that a cue for me to leave?"

"Hmm. Let me think," she said, a smile on her lips, her eyes fixed on him, amused by her little victory. She crossed her arms and rubbed them with her palms. "No, I think you better stay," she said. "I'll show you my place."

Samad was often struck by her direct manner. She was strong-willed, attractive and likable, different from the passive girls his mother wanted him to marry. She made him feel less in control than he would have liked, and this made him uncomfortable at times. For the moment, though, everything felt right, just as it ought to be. They took their wineglasses and went to the bedroom. Samad noticed flowers in a blue vase, Gauguin prints on the walls and a bookshelf full of paperbacks. Her makeup lay scattered on a dressing table. A half-opened drawer offered a glimpse of neatly layered clothes, in florals and shades of blues. She squeezed his hand and went over to the dressing table. Samad slumped into an armchair and watched as she undid her hair. They exchanged glances in the tall, oval mirror. Samad was falling, happy in this headlong descent. He knew that any moment she would come to him. This promise gave him an intoxicating feeling of power. It was a very agreeable feeling, this erotic excitement. As she came near, he drew her to him and inhaled the scent of her hair. Their eyes met for a second. Their fingers intertwined.

"What are you thinking?" she asked.

"Nothing," he said, lying. He was thinking of his desire for her. He trembled with anticipation as she put her arms around him. Then her mouth was pressing against his and there was no more room, no more light, nothing but the girl.

Hers was an unaffected, simple beauty. He loved her locutions and the way she inadvertently put a lilt at the ends of her sentences. He loved the way she sat in front of her mirror. He loved how, even after several months of intimacy, she would move out of sight to undress. He remembered the time she picked up an injured bird from the pavement in one deft motion, as only a woman who has spent time on farms can do. She had tears in her eyes when she realized that it was badly hurt and there was nothing to be done. Samad felt a great affection for her but he did not love her then. He had hoped their affair would be over in six months. In six months his mother would find him a suitable bride and he would be cured of Kate and she of him. But six months turned into a year and then another, and then he did not quite know how he would leave her. The only element to spoil the romance was the guilt of knowing that he was acting recklessly and against the wishes of his mother. At such moments, he felt that he was doing something dishonorable.

They lived in separate flats but Kate came over often and they went out on dates. They saw a new film nearly every week and, on weekends, they went on day trips around the hills and wineries of

Melbourne. Kate knew that he was unsure about her. When he talked to his mother on the phone, she could not understand what he was saying but she could sense what he was holding back. She introduced him to her parents; they disapproved, worried that he was a complete unknown and that she might leave, but she didn't care. She knew that she had to be patient with him, but she was prepared to wait. He needed time. It was going to take him a lot longer than her to know if he was in love. She was in no doubt that she loved him.

Samad kept the relationship secret from his mother until he had proposed to Kate. Until then, he let her search out prospective matches for him in Karachi and he went about meeting the girls on his visits home to keep up the pretense, weighed down by the double guilt of betraying his mother on one side and Kate on the other. Sometimes, he made lists in his head to weigh up the good and bad points of their relationship and calculate if theirs could be a happy marriage. If he married Kate, he upset his mother. If he didn't marry her, he appeased his mother, but at what price? There was still no guarantee that she could find him a wife who would make him happy. That was the problem. There was no peace for him. A price had to be paid, no matter what path he followed. Sooner or later he would have to make a choice between his mother's wishes and his own.

Kate was not surprised when he told her his mother had been showing him prospective wives on his visits home. He thought that she would be insulted and might even walk out on him but she was lighthearted and curious.

"Oh really?" she said. "What were they like?"

It became a joke between them. Each time he went to visit his mother, Kate asked if he was going to inspect any more girls. She did not like it, of course, that Samad was keeping her existence secret from his mother; it irritated her, and she found it deeply distressing that Mrs. Khan could go about planning an arranged marriage for Samad when he was with her. But despite her misgivings, she trusted him. She could sense that she was becoming dearer to him. She could see it in the way he looked at her and how he spoke to her. He was falling in love with her and everything else, his country, his culture, even his family, was becoming more distant.

Samad wrote to Bilqis saying that he was engaged. She was heartbroken when she received the letter and phoned him to say that she did not approve. It was as if everything she had hoped for and worked toward had been rendered null and void. When he visited her, Bilqis called him into her study and tried to persuade him to break up with Kate. He refused.

"You are asking me, your elderly mother, to get on a plane and meet your girlfriend? What for? Are you trying to tell me that she is better than all the girls I have shown you? Did you keep silent all this time so that you could insult me like this?"

"I am not insulting you, Mother," Samad said calmly. "I am telling you that I can't do this anymore. I can't let you keep looking when I know who I want to marry."

"You will suffer deeply," she told him.

"You are sorry because she is a foreigner?"

"I wouldn't put it that way, but it's not far from the truth," said Bilqis. "These women know how to attract men. They fall in and out of love all the time. It's just a game for them. No doubt they have pasts too, what with their boyfriends and so on. Their parents let them run wild. It's not like here. They are free, yes, but God preserve us if our girls start showing such levity. We would never permit it."

Samad stared at the floor in dismay. "I can see what kind of person she is," he said. "I have sense enough. Have you no faith in me?"

"I would not expect you to say anything else. Once the passion is gone, then you'll see the real person. She and you are separated by everything imaginable. Is she going to do the housework? Will she cook for you? I tell you, these women . . . the notion of equality has gone to their heads. I should like to know how a marriage is to survive when everyone wants to have their cake and eat it too. No wonder so many of their marriages end up in divorce. Why don't you ask her if she wants a career or children? Tell her that she can't have both and then see what she says."

"Mother, whoever said that I wanted to have a housemaid for a wife?"

"Do you think I was looking for a housemaid for you? Do you think I am so stupid that I don't even know what you want?"

"Lower your voice," Samad said. "The servants will hear us."

"Let them hear us," Bilqis cried angrily. "They are here for me. They obey me. They respect me. They should know what kind of son you are."

"That's enough!" Samad shouted. He rose and went into the kitchen to see if anyone was there. Mumtaz was there.

"What are you doing here?" Samad snapped. "Your work is done, isn't it? Why are you standing around? Are you eavesdropping?"

The girl trembled and then her face turned red. "I haven't been eavesdropping," she said. "I was going home. I was waiting to see . . ."

"Waiting to see what?"

"I was waiting to see if my begum needed me."

"Your begum does not need you," Samad said, sullied by her reply. "You can go."

She glared at him. She seemed even more indignant than he was. It was an awful feeling to be glared at by someone he had known since childhood, and particularly unbearable because it implied a familiarity as though between siblings except, of course, that the girl was a servant. He felt her power and was astonished at her nerve. He was grateful when she finally saw herself out. Bolting the door behind her, he marched back to the study.

Bilqis was sitting where he had left her. She had closed her eyes. "I remember your father used to say things of that sort," she said. "When I married him, he had just come back from England. I suppose that's why he married me, because I had been educated at a convent. I was a hybrid and he found that appealing. He was an Anglophile but at heart he wanted a traditional wife. In my entire life, I never saw him iron his shirts. He never changed your nappies. He never darned his socks. He expected women to do these things because that's how he was brought up. You think that you are going to be different but you are cut from the same cloth. You've been brought up the same way. People don't change, say what you will. You attach undue importance to the individual, when a woman is nothing without her people. I have no doubt that Kate has a great reserve of affection for you, but she draws her strength from her people. Let's bring her here and see how long she can sustain her affection for you. I wager she will pack her bags in a year."

"In a year?" Samad laughed.

"These women don't know the first thing about duty and sacrifice," Bilqis said. "They belong to another world. Their society is different. Their customs are different. The way they think is different. They're not of our kind."

"I am not asking her to live here."

Bilqis smiled. "I see. Gone forever, yes? It was a fait accompli anyway, but now the matter is settled. Very well then, go and live your life as you please; leave me to die alone."

Samad twisted in his chair. "Do you enjoy making me miserable?"

"On the contrary, it hurts me a great deal," said Bilqis, "but I say it as it is. I have lived longer than you. I have seen more of life than you and I am wiser than you. I have left you at your liberty, but that is not to say that I am indifferent to your actions. I believe I have a right to counsel you. I cannot forbid you to marry Kate, but if you do not take my advice, then I may at least tell you how I feel."

"You have made your feelings quite known to me."

"But you defy me, don't you?"

"I love her."

"It is the fatal attraction of the white race to the dark. There is nothing else to it."

Samad was furious now. Physical attraction was only the most obvious consideration. There were other considerations too. Kate was stronger than he, and her convictions ran deeper. He had vacillated and not trusted himself with confronting his mother but she went single-mindedly against her parents' wishes to be with him. Her faith in him was not only greater than his faith in her, it was greater than his faith in their love.

"You are obstinate and you do me an injustice," he said. "You ought to have stated your prejudices a long time ago, but never mind. I would have been sorry to hear them then, and I am sorry to hear them now. Frankly, if you did not wish me to mingle with people of other races, then why did you send me abroad?"

Bilqis looked up at him, maintaining a taciturn air. "It is all well to mingle with people of other races, but in times of trial it is only your own people who will stand by you. Birds of a feather."

"It takes courage to see the other side."

"And what makes you think that they will ever see our side?"

"Hope, Mother, hope! I am not a coward sticking my head in the sand."

"You are not a coward, you are a fool!" she cried. "Your father would be sorry to hear you speak to me like this."

Samad rose from his chair. He stared down at Bilqis for a moment and then he left the study and stormed out of the house. He walked down Clifton Road to Khayaban-e-Iqbal, and kept walking from the Teen Talwar roundabout with its three marble swords toward the old racecourse. He walked for nearly an hour until he found a tea shop that stayed open past midnight. There were always people near the railway station. A horse-drawn tonga stood under a tree, its driver curled asleep on his seat. A row of coolies squatted by the roadside waiting for passengers. Under a streetlamp, a barber lathered a man's beard with a shaving brush. As time went by, Samad started feeling sorry for treating his mother badly. His anger cooled and he walked back home. He drew a sense of restitution from having caused her pain because it caused him an equal measure of pain, but it gave him no satisfaction because the arguments damaged and humiliated them both. What was he meant to do? He had imagined himself to be called upon to do great things and he wanted to make a start by marrying the woman he loved, but something seemed amiss without his mother's consent. It was as if he were not his own master. His mother was directing his actions. He could realize his aspirations only with her blessing. Life became whole and complete only then, everything reconciled in one. Otherwise life was not life but the mechanics of life. How could this be so?

Samad had fond memories of his childhood. He was born and raised in Karachi and lived for most of his youth near Clifton Beach, or what used to be Clifton Beach, with its miles of open roads and marshes. To the north lay Saddar, Empress Market and the other bazaars in a maze of shops and houses that spread over many square miles. In those days, in the late sixties and early seventies, no part of Karachi was off-limits. It was a safe city then, and there was nothing so exciting as growing up there as a boy. He roamed the streets on his bicycle. His father had three brothers, two of whom lived within a few miles of Samad's family. Samad ate and slept in their houses, played with his cousins and ordered their servants about. They were open-minded and liberal people. No one paid much attention to religious matters, except for celebrating the festival of Eid, which provided an excuse for the adults to make their social visits and the children to collect presents.

After Samad turned twelve, he spent five years as a boarder at Lawrence College in Murree. The college was his father's alma mater, one of a handful of public schools that the British had built in India. Wealthy families sent their sons there to be groomed to become diplomats and heads of multinational companies. It boasted a cricket oval, mulberry trees and redbrick buildings. The senior boarders sat on high tables and presided over the other tables in the dining hall, eating with deliberate slowness to keep the others from fleeing. Time stood still there. The only sport that had gone out of fashion after the Partition was rugby, and although there were more curries on the menu than there used to be, the boys still had porridge for breakfast and tea and cake in the afternoon. Every morning, the gardeners pulled an iron roller over the cricket pitch. The lawns, hedges and rosebushes were always in immaculate trim. On weekends, the boys spit-polished their shoes, put on blue blazers and gray trousers and walked into town to catch sight of pretty girl boarders from the Convent of Jesus and Mary.

The quiet retreat in the Himalayan foothills was still an agreeable milieu then. It had escaped the vicissitudes that had altered the cities and retained much of its colonial air. The town of Murree lay on a four-mile-long ridge, seven thousand feet above sea level. The main boulevard was known as the "Mall" and the other roads had also kept their old English names. The shops were called emporiums. Their sign boards were written in English and their owners had not changed since the Partition. In the restaurants, with names like Sam's and Lintott's, the waiters were old soldiers from the disbanded British Indian army. They wore starched white uniforms and sported enormous handlebar mustaches that bristled with indignation if their customers did not look respectable. The town was perched at the edge of a small plateau that overlooked a beautiful valley shaped like an immense basin. Many of the buildings, such as the Cecil Hotel, were distinguished landmarks from the old days and lent the place a semblance not quite of England or of India but of somewhere in between, a sort of Edwardian idyll that existed quite outside of time.

Samad's parents visited him in summer to escape the Karachi heat. During these visits, he and his father often went on long, strenuous hikes together. Samad liked going on these hikes, as his father knew his way through the hills and gulleys and, each time he visited, showed him some track that Samad did not know about. After these expeditions, they climbed up the rickety stairs at Lintott's to reach the dark-paneled tearooms, where a waiter brought them cucumber sandwiches and tea. When Samad became a senior boarder, his father talked to him about what he might want to do after leaving school. He wanted him to have the best education. His academic achievements were excellent and his teachers spoke highly of him. Hashmat thought that going overseas was the right thing for him to do. The words made a deep impression on the young boy. Everything around him paled in comparison to the future that awaited him now. He studied harder than ever and thumbed reverently through brochures from foreign universities. He was only sixteen years old, but he could not wait to leave the country.

Samad's father was a lively man with a vast circle of friends whom he entertained lavishly. The son of an enlightened Indian Muslim family, Hashmat belonged to the category of men who realize too late that they are somehow not suited to their line of work, because their vocation lies elsewhere, and so they lead disenchanted, slightly embittered but brilliant lives. A lawyer by day, he wrote verse by night. A publisher friend printed small runs of his poems and made up for the loss with the sale of pulp magazines. It was his father's rich and varied career that Samad would measure his own life by.

In contrast, Bilqis was a stern and formal mother, who had old-fashioned notions of how children should be brought up. For her, Samad's course in life was so defined that there was no further opportunity for him, no need, in fact, to think matters over and ask why things had to be one way and not another. She'd had the highest expectations of him at school, then there was the emphasis on profession, career and respectability. She'd assumed that Samad's betrothal to some elegant young lady was a foregone conclusion. This was how he perceived her through his adolescence into adulthood. By the time Samad was sent to boarding school, the family was beginning to disperse. Most of his cousins were sent to Europe and America for schooling and one by one their parents also moved overseas.

When his father died, Samad inwardly blamed his mother for the loss. He persuaded himself that her domineering spirit had killed him. It was a perverse logic, but the more he saw her through adult eyes, the more she came to represent the opposite of what he imagined his father to be. Everything about her provoked in him a need to defend his own individuality.

6

"THERE IS A lot of show, I must warn you," Samad told Kate before the reception. "This is not one of those functions you have back at home, all muted and restrained. There will be hundreds of people, all dressed to the nines. They have a taste for pomp and spectacle, and my mother is certain to orchestrate an effect." Samad had been tutoring her for weeks, ever since their own, rather plain, wedding ceremony in Melbourne. To these people, first impressions mattered most, he had said. Everything was about form and poise, and manners and status accounted for a great deal. Kate was determined to give a most splendid account of herself, but nothing he said could have prepared her for that warm spring night's gathering.

Bilqis, the newlyweds and the rest of the family were standing on the porch of the Sind Club to receive guests. Darkness fell quickly after the sun went down. A ribbon of orange light fading above the horizon was all that remained. The palms swayed in the breeze. It was warm and pleasant. Kate could hear the traffic trundling down Abdullah Haroon Road, or Victoria Road, as most people called it. The perimeter wall of the Sind Club blocked her view of the outside world, sheltering her from the eyesore of sputtering auto rickshaws, tongas and buses. Even the ever-present flies seemed not to dare enter these hallowed grounds of manicured gardens and Victorian buildings.

Car after car turned into the long driveway, gliding up to the porch and dislodging their well-dressed occupants. Amid the rustling silks and the soft tinkling of bangles, women climbed up the short flight of stairs to greet Bilqis and Kate with kisses. Kate wore a red gharara and dainty golden sandals with straps. The heavy skirtlike dress over her pants was hand-embroidered with gold stitching along the edges and patterns of beaded flowers and little petals woven around them. A thin linen shawl with gold edging was pinned to her hair. Her hands were painted with henna, and her arms were laden with heavy bracelets of gold. Her dark hair and milky skin were set off by the dress. The men bowed politely at the ladies, a few of the bolder ones shook hands with Kate—and, she, of course, extended her hand if they offered theirs, spoke only when spoken to and smiled graciously at their witticisms. If the guests offered her presents, as they invariably did, she politely declined at first, as instructed, waiting for the guests to insist, and then accepted. After exchanging a few words with their hosts, the guests filed into the grand saloon and the hosts turned to greet the next arrivals.

"There goes the Chief Justice," Sikander remarked to Kate as they started making their way inside. The last of the guests, a tall, gray-haired man, had just walked past. "The *old* Chief Justice," he said, in a tone that was at once revering and possessive. "Always calls a spade a spade. Resigned his post not a day after the Hudood Laws were passed. He's not one of those fellows rallying to serve the junta. Told General Zia that they were ultra vires of the constitution and against all that is secular and reasonable. Very forthright and straight, I might say. Zia was furious."

"The rape laws, you mean?" asked Kate.

Sikander nodded. "They were the first of the Sharia laws," he said, although he seemed sorry for having mentioned them in the first place. Kate had not only comprehended his words but echoed back, by the tone of her voice and by her expression, how distasteful the whole thing was to her. He looked at her with a mixture of indulgence and reproach, as if she were not meant to be judging these things, which were never as simple as they seemed. Touching her elbow lightly, Sikander ushered her into the saloon toward a group of beckoning guests.

The grand saloon was white, with tall windows, polished-brass knobs on the doors, large potted plants in the corners and crystal chandeliers on the ceiling. Waiters in red turbans and white starched uniforms glided through the air-conditioned hall, bearing trays with iced beverages. The bride and groom now stood in the midst of guests. The ladies were resplendent in saris of emerald green, turquoise and white, with gold earrings and pearl necklaces, and the men, elderly but turned out in fine dinner jackets, carried themselves as gentlemen. Even the children had perfect self-possession. They were utterly well behaved, and they mirrored the poise of their elders. Kate had the impression that she had stepped into a soiree that Jean Béraud might have painted.

On long tables decked with white linen, there were mountains of steaming pilau, burnished gold and speckled with cardamom and saffron. Skewers of kebabs, glistening and hot, dripped with exquisite juices and sizzled on beds of charcoal. There were piles of naan bread, cauldrons of kofta and chicken curry, and crate loads of soft drinks, supplied with straws and napkins wrapped around the glass bottles.

The guests ate amid the tinkling of cutlery and muted conversation. The plates were white bone china and the service was silver. There was no lack of appetite. Shahid devoured his koftas, his relish apparent in the beads of perspiration on his forehead. Even Sikander had ignored his manners and curled his fingers around a greasy chicken bone. He stood in the center of the room, towering over his compatriots, chatting merrily and infecting the place with his booming laughter.

He told tales, in his own peculiar blend of opinion and fact, which never sounded dull and were far more entertaining than the commonplace talk. In the summer of the previous year, he had slipped into Afghanistan to cover the Russian war. He rode on horseback from Garam Chashma over the unguarded mountain pass, which was the traditional route used by lapis lazuli smugglers. Ahmad Shah Massoud, the Tajik commander, hosted him in his own house. A photograph he passed around was of himself standing with Massoud next to a roadside restaurant called the Islamic Hotel. Its name was scrawled in white paint on the turret of a burned-out Russian tank.

"A truckload of his mujahideen nearly forced me off the road into a minefield. It was their idea of fun. Had I not pulled my horse up hard, I would have been blown to bits."

He lamented how he had to pray with them and was not permitted to smoke his cigarettes, but there were sublime moments too, such as when he saw the lights of Russian towns twinkling across the Amu Darya. Gallant raconteur, he paid his friends' wives little compliments, diminished them here, elevated them there. He drew them out and made them laugh. His descriptions of the Afghan countryside, its enamel-blue skies, the cedar-covered mountains crowned with white snow and the sight of peasant girls in long red frocks, bearing water flasks on their heads, appealed to their feminine sensibilities. It was all harmless, innocuous banter. They teased him and flirted with him in front of their husbands. The fact that he was not quite like their husbands, he was far too brilliant and too intellectual, made him dangerous and charming, and they could imagine him to be everything that their husbands were not.

"I ought to show you the rest of the club one day," Sikander said, turning to Kate. "There is a swimming pool at the back. At the end of the corridor, there is an old weighing machine. You'll find its note-book has entries going back to the thirties. We also have a modest library upstairs and there is, of course, the billiards room. It's gather-ing dust these days. Without the booze, no one cares to play."

"He wants to impress you with his hunting trophies there," Bilqis said, glancing at Kate.

"Well, it's a matter of fact." Sikander shrugged, perfectly mod-est. "You may see them, that is if one of the bearers hasn't sold them to the scrap dealers already. The bearers here are deucedly indif-ferent now, you see. One does not know them. In my day, the men were picked from the old regiments. They took pride in what they did. It's a damn shame to see the place fall to pieces, but I may tell you, in the matter of game and scenery, this country is still match-less. I have been up in the Himalayas from one end to the other and I have seen the Alps and whatnot, and I daresay that from Skardu to Chitral lie the grandest, most magnificent mountains in the world."

Kate listened with attentive silence. The affluence of the party had put her into greater confusion than before. She had watched films about India, and read many novels set in the colonial times, to get immersed in the culture of the subcontinent. She had friends who had returned from India exultant and transformed, but Pakistan was different. She remembered the first time she told her friends about her new Pakistani boyfriend. The news wasn't well received. They looked at her strangely.

"Nothing good has ever come from a country with a 'stan' in its name," one of them said.

"Except for cricket," said another.

"Is he good-looking, like Imran Khan?" one of the girls asked.

Kate could have so easily felt insulted but she remembered only a feeling of profound disappointment. She knew that her friends meant her well. They just did not understand why someone like her was going out with a foreigner with God knows what dark secrets and strange customs when she could have had any decent Australian man she liked. The fact was that no one knew much about Pakistan. People looked at her with a mixture of curiosity and dismay when she told them that she was going there. Wasn't it some sort of failed nation-state given over to dictators and mullahs? What was she going there for? A husband? Nervous smiles and silence.

But instead of skull-cap-wearing fanatics and veiled women in black, Kate had met elegant and handsome people, tall and refined like old-fashioned Italians except that there was a degree of solemnity about their features, a cast that was at once noble and wild, not subdued. Their complexions were surprisingly fair, their countenance formal and austere. They had dark, glittering, unwavering eyes and severe but graceful expressions. There was something else about them, something dangerous that had been restrained within. Perhaps it was nothing more than a fancy of hers that some of the gray-haired gentlemen in the assembly had the same hawkish features she had seen once in a charcoal pencil drawing of a band of Pathan tribesmen about to ambush a column of English Redcoats.

As the guests broke away into groups, Kate and Samad's cousin Zainab found themselves standing next to each other. She was tall and pale and had the high cheekbones of her aunt, which made her seem a little haughty, but underneath she was girlish and bubbly. She had never been abroad, she told Kate. Having formed her impressions from fashion magazines and films, she was curious to find out the truth from a real Westerner.

"How did you two meet?" she asked.

"At an office party."

"We have tea parties here. General Zia has put a ban on parties. He is a puritan, you see. He wants to save us from hell. He won't even let us see a couple holding hands on television. They have to make do by looking longingly at each other."

Kate gave her a smile. "Do men and women meet at tea parties?"

Zainab giggled. "Well, that can happen, but you have to watch out for the police. If they catch you on a date, they'll want proof that you are married—otherwise they can arrest you. Since they are useless at catching the real criminals, that's what they do now."

"That doesn't sound like much fun."

"Fun—what's that word?" Zainab remarked. "It's not in my dictionary."

Kate liked the girl. She was feisty and unapologetic, not afraid of anyone.

"Can I ask you something?" Zainab asked sweetly.

"Of course."

"What is it like to have free sex?"

"What do you mean?" Kate burst out laughing.

"I mean, what is it like to live in a society where girls and boys sleep with each other and no one thinks twice about it?"

"There isn't that much free sex going around, actually."

"I don't believe you," Zainab said.

"Some of my girlfriends haven't had sex for a long time."

"Why not?"

"They don't have boyfriends."

"Don't they have casual sex? Don't they go to discos and pick up?"

"Not my friends," Kate said.

Zainab appeared incredulous, as if that was not what she had expected.

"How are they going to get married then?" she asked.

"They'll have to meet someone they really like. It's not easy to meet people you like. It gets harder as your friends get married and the circle of eligible partners becomes smaller and smaller, because the people who would otherwise introduce you lose interest in you; and, once they have children, they're so preoccupied with themselves that their single friends have no hope of being matched up with someone else."

"But your girlfriends are not virgins?"

"No, they're not."

Zainab seemed content with this answer as if, at least, this supposition had not been proved false. A silence followed. Kate sensed that Zainab was weighing another question.

"Did you have boyfriends before you met Samad?"

"I had a couple," Kate remarked. "Why, have you?"

"No, never," said Zainab, triumphant.

Kate did not mind being interrogated—Zainab's questions were genuine and she was asking them innocently—but she was offended by the prejudice that was apparent in every question. When Zainab said that she could not wait to get out of the country, Kate looked at her with disbelief. Why would she want to get out of the country if the West was so decadent? Where would she go? What for?

Zainab said that she wanted to paint. She felt it was her vocation to paint but her parents thought it was a whim. They wanted her to get married, and regularly issued dire warnings that she could not afford not to entertain proposals. A few years seemed like forever, they said, but time passed in a flash and finding a suitable boy would only become more and more difficult. Zainab then launched into a long and fierce argument in favor of love marriages.

She leaned forward. "If my aunt had her way, I would have ended up marrying Samad."

Kate laughed, although the revelation made her uncomfortable.

"I couldn't marry him because he is like my brother," Zainab continued. "I'll only marry someone I love. It's all changing now. More and more girls are rebelling against their families and opting for love marriages. Why should I have an arranged marriage when my parents had a love marriage themselves?"

"Would you consider marrying a European man?" Kate asked.

"No."

"What if he converted to Islam?"

She shook her head again.

"It's out of the question," she said.

Kate was disappointed. She had tried to find common ground with Zainab. There seemed something so natural in her remarks that she thought that they understood each other. Now she perceived that, for all her talk, her perkiness was not habitual, but a rare outburst of defiance. For all her rant about love marriages, Zainab would ultimately defend her repression and even use language to justify it. The possibility of considering someone of another culture and race, of ever breaking the mold, was closed to her. They were not alike at all.

"The air is like steam here," declaimed an ironic voice beside them.

Kate turned to see Mahbano fanning herself with her hand. Her face looked flushed. Kate thought that she had probably overheard their conversation. She wondered what Zainab's mother was going to say to her. Was there going to be another interrogation?

"Can we do something about the air-conditioning?" Mahbano remarked, looking at Zainab.

Zainab excused herself.

Mahbano watched her daughter as she made her way through the crowd of people. "Do you like it here?" she asked, turning to Kate.

Kate made some innocuous comment about how courteous and hospitable everyone had been. Mahbano brushed her off.

"It is just form," she said flatly. "We oblige others so that they may oblige us. You must be honest. How can you like it? It is so very dull."

"I wish it were dull," Kate remarked. "This morning, I spent two hours at the hairdresser's and three hours at the beautician's. I spent all of the afternoon getting dressed. I haven't had a moment's rest."

"Here, let me look at your hands. My, what beautiful patterns you have there! Who put it on?"

"Mumtaz. I had to sit still holding out my hands like this," Kate said, gesturing. "I wasn't allowed to read a book or even eat."

"Mumtaz could have held up a book for you," Mahbano said, chuckling. "She could have fed you too, with a spoon. Come now, you only get pampered like this once. What are you sulking about? Just be glad that you're not having a formal wedding here. This is only a reception. If you think this is bad, our weddings are ten times worse. One day you will look back and laugh at it."

"I know," Kate said. "I shouldn't complain. It's just that I don't like others doing things for me."

"Maybe you are not used to it."

"There are some things I can never get used to."

"Such as?"

"Such as someone doing my makeup."

"You didn't do it yourself?"

"No, I wasn't allowed. The beautician did it for me."

"I think you look luminous."

"I've got too much foundation on."

"You look fine."

"I can feel it caked on my face."

"I've seen brides who were twice as made up as you are. They loved it. Didn't you like dressing up when you were a little girl?"

"Yes."

"Well, then, think of yourself as a little girl again. You went to Sarafa bazaar, I presume?"

"Yes."

"Did you like it?"

"Yes."

"Good. I am pleased to hear it. It's a woman's paradise. Jewelry shops, hundreds of them, some no bigger than a hole in the wall, all scattered in a labyrinth of narrow alleys. Now, you won't see something like that in Australia, will you?"

"Quite extraordinary, I thought."

"I could spend my whole life there. I love jewelry. I can never get enough of it. I suppose you like gold?"

"I prefer silver, actually."

"What about rubies?"

"I like diamonds."

Mahbano laughed. Kate was draped in gold. A choker with a pendant inlaid with a dozen small rubies hung around her neck. Heavy gold earrings drooped down to her shoulders. A diamond-shaped tikka inlaid with rubies dangled over her forehead. Mahbano thought how pretty she was—how pretty and how exacting, even in circumstances quite beyond her control, and bridling, just a little, when things did not go her way. Did she realize that the reception was not about her? It was about people's expectations of her. It did not matter what she liked and disliked. It did not matter what she said and what she thought. What mattered was how people perceived her. Gold suited her fine. It suited the circumstances.

"Tell me about your wedding in Australia," Mahbano said. "What was it like? What did you wear? Who came? I want to know everything."

Kate was beginning to warm to Mahbano. This elegant, heavy-set woman seemed like a lighter version of her austere sister.

"Well, I wore a white dress," she said, "but it wasn't a wedding dress. It was just an ordinary dress that Samad and I found in a boutique. He liked it so I bought it. He wore a tailor-made suit but I chose the tie for him. We invited about fifty people. We could have invited another fifty but we wanted to keep it small. It wasn't easy, though. Some people don't take it well if they don't get invited. In the end, we only invited my family, Samad's mother, of course, and our close friends. I had to leave out some of my cousins who I hadn't seen for years."

"Wonderful! And were you married in a church?"

"Oh no." Kate chuckled. "Samad wouldn't have allowed that and I cannot imagine what Mrs. Khan would have done. We were married in a restaurant by the seaside. A celebrant came to take our vows and then we all had dinner. We didn't even have any speeches."

"You have speeches?" Mahbano frowned.

"Yes, my father wanted to say a few words about me and wish us luck, but he gets a bit sentimental after a few drinks, so we banned him. He didn't like that."

Mahbano laughed again. "I am sure everyone had a nice time," she said.

"Did Mrs. Khan say anything?" Kate asked.

"No, but she didn't complain either, which is praise in itself."

"I am glad."

"It must seem very different here," Mahbano said. "What do you make of it all?"

Kate nodded. "I feel that I'm always being judged. A lot is expected of me but I don't quite know what it is because so much is left unsaid. I suppose that I do a lot of things that a Pakistani girl would never do."

"Like what?"

"I don't know. If I knew, I wouldn't be saying this to you."

Mahbano touched the fabric of Kate's dress and rubbed it between her fingers. "You are a curiosity, an object of wonder," she said. "It is not every day that a young man of good family marries a pretty foreigner. People want to see what stuff you are made of, what thoughts you think, the way you talk. They are bored. They need their excitement. Your background, the circumstances that brought you two together and the fate of mixed marriages are topics so rife for speculation that people cannot help themselves."

"What is the fate of mixed marriages?"

"Well, it's like the bird and the fish who fall in love. You are the bird, and we the fish, coming to have a look at this heavenly creature who has managed to snare one of ours."

"Isn't that a fairy tale about doomed lovers?"

"That's if you believe in fairy tales."

"Mrs. Khan wants me to settle in Pakistan."

"And would you?"

Kate gave her a stricken look.

"Ah, she said something, didn't she?" Mahbano remarked. "Come, tell me, what did she say?"

Kate had not expected a direct question. She tried to be tactful. "Oh, many things. I asked her if she would migrate to Australia. She said that she would not want to live anywhere else except here. She said that if I spent a year with her, I'd know what she meant. I feel that I've done her a terrible disservice. She had expected to live a certain kind of life and then I came along and upset all her plans. Had Samad married—"

Mahbano pressed the girl's hand in hers. "Shh now—not a word more," she said. "My sister likes to test people. She likes to know where they stand so she knows where she stands in relation to them. It's her defense. It gives her peace of mind. I would do the same, if I were in her position—alone, I mean. You should not be cross with her."

Kate blinked away tears and looked searchingly at Mahbano. "I've heard about you," she said.

"Have you?"

"Samad speaks fondly of you. He told me how you went against family wishes to marry your husband. He says you are the family rebel."

"Yes, well, I am not sure if that's true," Mahbano said with a laugh. "You ought not to pay attention to everything that people say."

"Tell me what happened."

"It's such a long time ago."

"Don't tell me if you don't want to."

Mahbano looked around at the guests. Her sister was standing near Sikander, her back toward them.

"When I was a girl, I used to sing," she said, looking at Kate again. "We had been in Pakistan a few years and I used to go on air. I didn't have any aspirations, but I had a nice voice and I liked singing. I met Shahid at the radio station. He was a singer too. We used to sing duets together. You wouldn't think of it now, but in those days he wasn't religious. He had long sideburns and he was a smart dresser. This was shortly after my father had passed away.

"Bilqis and Hashmat were already married and, since I was a single girl, I lived in their house. Bilqis wanted to set me up with one of Hashmat's friends, but I couldn't get along with any of them. I was in love with Shahid. We were both deeply in love. We used to say to each other that if our families did not permit us to get married, we'd elope and live our lives in the mountains somewhere, tucked away in a snowbound village, where nobody would ever be able to find us. My sister was greatly opposed. She thought that Shahid was not a worthy match and that I was marrying below my station. She used to tell me all sorts of horror stories of love marriages that had gone wrong. She even dragged me to an astrologist once to have my horoscope read. He told me that if I married Shahid, I would die within months. But of course nothing could persuade me to change my mind. We got married and moved to Lahore and she did not talk to me for a year."

"But you made up with her?"

"Oh, of course," Mahbano said. "I wasn't going to keep her away from me. She's my sister. I love her. I didn't mind what she said because it went in through one ear and out the other. I always did what I pleased."

"Is that your advice?"

Mahbano was wistful now. Memories of the past danced before her eyes. "If you take my advice, you should do as you like and let things be," she said. "The world will turn. It always does."

7

THE RECEPTION CONTINUED past nine o'clock. The guests were finishing their dessert as the waiters brought out the tea. Bilqis had joined a cluster of glittering ladies. Conversation droned around her. One woman wondered if the wallpaper her daughter had sent from London suited the draperies in her bedroom. Another lamented the weight of textbooks her grandsons were carrying to school. Displaying great emotion in the noble cause of charity, the governor's wife spoke for many minutes about her horror at the plight of beggar children. Then followed a discussion of Sydney Pollack's *Out of Africa*, which had won seven Oscars. One of the guests remarked that a great director needs to vindicate himself only once. It does not matter how many bad films he makes as long as he makes one that is memorable. From the merits of the year's crop of Oscar contenders, the chitchat digressed into fond reminiscences about the times when, for a rupee and eight annas, one could sit on a sofa in the balcony of Paradise Cinema in downtown Karachi and watch Richard Burton take Elizabeth Taylor in his arms.

Bilqis was only half listening, distracted by a conversation nearby, where the men were speaking of the latest Indian maneuvers along the Line of Control in the disputed state of Kashmir. Sikander had written a column speculating that this was in response to Pakistani-trained fighters infiltrating Indian Kashmir. If the infiltrations did not stop, he had written, India would launch all-out war on Pakistan.

"The Indians won't attack, say what you will," Shahid said. "If they attack, we will counterattack. I have it on reliable authority that Indian tank regiments near the Sialkot border are short of fuel. Our air force will put them out of action in no time. Then we will send a signal to the Kashmiri insurgents. They will be waiting and, as soon as the command is given"—he snapped his fingers—"they will block all roads and bridges. Our fighters will have a clear path to Srinagar. And once we have Srinagar, the Indians can't take it back."

"And who is going to broker a peace?" Sikander asked.

"The Americans," Shahid said.

"Our steadfast friends?"

Shahid sipped his tea and shrugged. "As long as the Russians are bogged down in Afghanistan, the Americans won't let anyone touch us. Not the Indians, not the Israelis, no one. Time is on our side. We can do what we please."

"But when they leave, we'll be on our own again."

"We have always been on our own," Shahid said, with perfect equanimity. "What makes you think that we ever had allies? Muslims have no allies. We have never had any allies. The Christians and Jews are our natural foes. They've come to dominate the world because we are weak. They will see to it that we never rise."

Murmurs of assent rose from the gathered men as they recollected, with the bitterness of people who know that the world has passed them by, how the nation of Islam had been a victim of Jewish rapaciousness, English perfidy and American pragmatism.

"War, gentlemen, will be forced upon us," Shahid said, finger pointing skyward. "Its logic is really quite simple. Europe and

America depend on oil, and the Muslims have it. They lecture us about democracy and human rights but they don't give a hoot about us. All they care about is our oil. When Mosaddeq nationalized the Iranian oil industry, the CIA replaced him with the Shah. When Nasser nationalized the Suez Canal, the British bombed him. How can they say that they care about democracy and human rights and then interfere with us and dominate us? No one says 'Boo!'—no one, not even our own rulers, who come to power only to loot and plunder until the next lot comes along. But how long will our people tolerate this outrage? Our generation might have put up with it, but our children are not going to. When they grow up, they will take the fight into their own hands. You will see. The system is condemned to fail. It will come to a fight."

Bilqis was furious at Shahid's remark. Kate and Mahbano were standing nearby, still talking. Bilqis glanced at them and sighed with relief, as they seemed not to have heard him. The usurper! How dare he talk about war with the West at a reception where the bride was a Westerner? Was Kate an enemy too? Her son had married her. Were his children going to be enemies too?

She turned her glare again at Shahid, who was still addressing his congregation. She could not believe that he had made the remark unwittingly. When he caught her eye, he smiled. All of a sudden, her old misgivings affirmed themselves. This was how he and his ilk were taking over the country, by insinuation and subterfuge, chipping away little by little at everything that was decent and civilized. Victory would be theirs if she acquiesced in silence. But she wasn't going to. This was her night. This was her celebration, and nobody was going to spoil it. If anyone wanted to see where she stood, she was going to show them right now.

The next moment, Kate noticed Bilqis beside her, looking imperious in her white sari and pearl necklace. Bilqis could not bring herself to say anything but she smiled and, for a brief moment, Kate found herself in a tight embrace, which left her with a sensation of silk, soft flesh and a whiff of Chanel.

"Well, sir, now that you've made the biggest mistake of your life, make sure you don't make any more."

The voice was taunting and familiar. Samad drew a short breath. He had been assailed by all sorts of questions tonight. People had wanted to know if Kate had become a Muslim and what her new name was. One lady asked whether the couple would circumcise boys, if they had boys. Yes, he had heard himself say with a plastic smile each time, yes, she had converted, yes, he would circumcise the boys, yes, yes—but this latest offense was really beyond the pale. He turned around to confront his accuser but found himself looking at an old friend, Asim, from his school days. He hadn't expected to see him and he instantly forgot his rancor.

"You devil! What the hell are you doing here?"

They embraced and shook hands. There was a good deal of backslapping and catching up on gossip. They spoke of mutual friends, compared predictions and passed verdicts about where everyone had ended up. They recalled the time when Samad was sixteen or seventeen and he used to go with Asim and his friends to his father's beach hut on Hawkes Bay. They would go there for the weekend, listen to The Doors and the Rolling Stones, play cards and flirt with Asim's female cousins and their girlfriends. Asim and Samad laughed with the abandon that is the prerogative of childhood friends, but from time to time, they looked at each other as if taking the measure of the man the other had become. Asim was working with a venture-capital firm on Wall Street. He was single and rich. He loved his work and talked about the deals he had done. The silences began to lengthen. It was a strange feeling to be speaking after being out of touch for years.

"What did you mean by 'mistake'?" Samad asked.

Asim looked at him blankly. He had already forgotten the jibe. When he recognized that he had inflicted a blow, a faint but sardonic smile appeared on his face.

"Oh come," he said, his eyes gleaming. "What are you looking at me like that for? I only meant it as a joke. Marriage, of course, my man. Tying the knot, slipping that ring on your finger, that sort of thing."

"Marrying a white girl, you mean?" Samad pressed.

Asim smirked. "The truth is, if there was anyone in our class who could pull it off, it was going to be you. You were always different, a freethinker. Only you could go against the grain. We didn't have the guts for it. You did. I knew it the moment I met you."

"And how about you?" Samad asked. "Found anyone yet?"

"Still looking," Asim said.

"Haven't your parents scoured the whole country by now?"

"They can't seem to find my kind of woman."

"What's this woman supposed to be like?"

"Oh well, she is not to be buck-toothed, four-eyed or hunched. That's been their haul so far. She has to be attractive and feminine, and she has to look after the house, look after me and look after our children. Simple. No confusion about roles. No nonsense about wanting to have it all."

Asim glanced around the room. "I say, there are more pretty girls here than my parents have shown me since they started looking," he said. He placed his hands on Samad's shoulders. "By the way, nice-looking girl, your wife," he said. "She must have something the others didn't, eh?"

The two friends used to swap stories of their sexual conquests when they had just gone overseas, in their first and second year of undergraduate studies. Asim's remark reminded Samad of those boasts, and he regretted ever having said such things.

"Well, you better do something before your hair falls out," he said. He jabbed a finger into his friend's noticeable paunch and felt grateful that he was in good shape himself.

"Toupees cost three thousand dollars."

"You've got it all figured out, then," Samad said with a laugh. He wondered if Asim still wanted a virgin bride.

"Girlfriend?"

Asim nodded. He took a cup of tea from a passing waiter and sipped at it.

"White?"

"I don't date any other race."

"Nice?"

"A little blonde, very nice."

Samad felt a pang of jealousy. Asim's relationships were purely physical. He was very up-front with his girls and never led them on, but he always managed to attract the prettiest ones.

"How long have you been going out?"

"Six months, maybe a bit more."

"That's quite a while," Samad said, hoping that he might be in love.

There was an awkward silence. Asim tapped the rim of his teacup with the spoon.

"It's not serious. I am just having a bit of fun."

Samad expected him to say as much. It was the sort of remark they used to make about white women—goddesses and whores, who were to be admired for their beauty and grace but reviled for their sexual ease.

Meanwhile the guests were starting to leave. The saloon emptied and the hubbub came to an end. Samad brooded about his own departure. He said his good-byes with mixed feelings. He had circulated among the guests, talked to them and laughed with them. Everyone had congratulated him, everyone had been courteous and polite, but his pleasure had been tainted by the feeling that time was passing rapidly. He did not want them to leave because he could not be part of their future, and he was already becoming a part of their past.

It was then that the realization struck him that he had broken a fundamental law. He had always enjoyed a Western aesthetic of beauty, but now he understood what most people in the room felt: that there was something cold and hard about white beauty. The same fair skin and fair hair that he found so alluring represented something coarse and half formed in their minds. While they valued fair skin, they did so only among their own kind. It all came down to a prejudice about beauty. No, it came down to a notion of superiority about themselves. They felt technically inferior to the West and physically too, perhaps, in the matter of appearance and general prowess, but morally they believed that they were better, and that was all that mattered.

Samad knew that there was something wrong in this self-righteousness, this smug contempt for the "other," as if the realm beyond their own people belonged to a diminished humanity. It was for this reason that he had secretly delighted at the prospect of challenging and offending, of lacerating their hypocrisy and flinging defiance at their archaic prejudices. Now he saw how precarious this notion of love against all odds actually was. He had fallen out of the orbit of his people. He had forfeited the peace of mind that comes from choosing the natural and easy path, in exchange for a life that he would constantly have to justify and rationalize. Marrying a foreigner would define him not only as an individual, but as someone who had given up his customary allegiances for the sake of love. And, in a moment of terrifying clarity, he understood that in his defiance of tradition he had let go of something essential.

PART 2

8

BILQIS AWOKE IN the dark to the sound of the telephone ringing. Murmuring prayers, she slipped on her robe and went downstairs. It was April. A year had gone by since the reception. The weather was turning warm again. Sweltering heat lay ahead. In Melbourne, Kate was pregnant and Bilqis was following the news from afar. She was excited at the prospect of becoming a grandmother. There was something reassuring in the thought that a part of her was going to live on after she was gone. But there was also an irony in this agreeable feeling, because the mother of her grandchild was the same woman she had not wanted her son to marry. She tried not to dwell on these thoughts because Kate was a nice person, a thoroughly good sort. She was honest and candid and far less circumspect than Samad. She wrote to Bilqis and called her on the telephone. She talked about everyday things with her, the sort of domestic minutiae—what they cooked, where they went, what they bought, and so on—that Samad never bothered to mention. Bilqis had become fond of her, as she was fond of Shahid, out of necessity and lack of choice, but sometimes she still seemed to her a complete stranger, alien and unfamiliar.

Bilqis turned on the light at the bottom of the stairs and lifted the receiver. She heard Samad's voice.

"Hello, hello? Is everything all right?"

There was a slight delay.

"It's a girl!"

"And everything is all right?"

"All's well."

A wave of relief swept over her. "Thank God!" Bilqis exclaimed.

She pulled up a chair by the telephone and began interrogating Samad. When did the contractions start? How long was the labor? When did they go to the hospital? Samad gave her an account as best as he could. There was a lot of interference on the line so he hung up and called again. The questions resumed. How much did the baby weigh? What did it feel like to hold her? Where was he when the baby came?

"You were there?" Bilqis laughed, shocked and amused. She had not imagined that Samad would have gone into the delivery ward of his own accord because it was a such a modern thing to do and totally out of character, and she wondered if he had been coaxed into it by his wife. If that were true, then it did not seem right to her because good wives did not bully or bend their husbands to their will, but she could not bring herself to ask him because he would defend Kate and accuse her of meddling.

"I wish you were here," Samad said.

"May God keep you," Bilqis replied, drawing herself from her thoughts. She was surprised at how much she missed him. "I'll be there soon enough. Have you given her a name yet?"

"We're going to call her Tara."

"What about a Muslim name?"

"It is a Muslim name."

"I mean something more traditional, like Rabab."

"Children will call her 'Rhubarb.'"

"Fatima is a nice name."

"Mother . . ." Samad sighed.

"Shall I sacrifice a goat in thanks?"

"It makes no difference to me."

"Well, is everything a matter of complete indifference to you? All children born into our family have had the aqeeqa done in the traditional way. The baby's head is shaved and silver the weight of its hair given away to the poor."

"You do as you please."

"Will you cut her hair?"

"I'll have to talk to Kate."

"Tell her that a child whose parents haven't made the offering falls prey to the evil eye. You are just like your father not to know these things."

"Yes, I remember," Samad said, as he hung up.

Bilqis went upstairs and lay down on her bed. She had been planning to go to Australia for the child's birth, but in the winter she had become ill. The doctors prohibited her from flying until her condition improved. It was her annual bout of flu, nothing unusual in that, except this time it was worsened by a touch of bronchitis. Her poor health exacerbated other, dormant symptoms. She had been tormented by stomach ulcers for years after her husband died. She thought that she had been cured of them but the pain had come back. Her belly felt like a drum, bloated and tight, although all tests were negative.

There was nothing to worry about, the doctors said. And what about the symptoms? Ah yes, she worried too much, they told her. She was too anxious, she needed to relax. With care in her diet she would be all right, except that the care proved most difficult. She was told to avoid things cooked in ghee. Helpings of sugar and syrupy desserts were cut back. Chilies and pickles were disallowed. Only yogurt and skim milk were permitted. Sago was especially recommended and so was fleawort seed laced with honey. Progressively, over a number of months, her diet became abstemious. The pain subsided, but she became weak.

The doorbell rang and brought her out of her reverie. It was now just after dawn. The chores of her day had begun. She made her bed and went downstairs. The milkman was talking to Mumtaz at the gate.

"Back to work, girl," Bilqis said to her lightly. "You gossip too much!"

The sweeper who cleaned outdoors came next. A dark, reedy-looking man, he grinned sheepishly when Bilqis opened the door.

"Where have you been?" she demanded.

"Sick," he replied.

Bilqis felt angry as the uncouth man went about his work without lifting his head. "A fine excuse, sickness," she said, "but you look in good health. The gutters overflowed and flooded my garden. What was I supposed to do?"

"The municipality sent others, didn't it?"

It was true. The municipality did send a contingent of sweepers to clean up the mess, but instead of cleaning the gutters they went about sweeping the lawn, and making neat little piles of leaves, broken branches and wet stumps of grass and mud. Afterward they sat down and smoked cheroots. One of the women even waved her thistle broom in Bilqis's face when she reprimanded her for the shoddy work. "What will you do, eh?" she rose, screaming, as she rolled up her sleeves and stood with her hands on her ample hips, seemingly enjoying Bilqis's powerlessness, suspecting that if Bilqis had any real power she would not have been standing there. "You want to file a complaint? Well, go ahead. What are you waiting for? The sweepers are with me. I'll tell them to dump the neighbors' shit in your grounds. There'll be shit everywhere. Shit on the walls and shit on the windows. Then what will you do?"

The unpleasant episode still rattled her. She did not like it when servants were rude. They were meant to behave themselves, but the sweepers were a belligerent lot. It was no use reasoning with them because they became abusive and foul-mouthed at the slightest pretext. The best thing was to deny them attention, because in reality they were defenseless. Their masters only had to ignore them to cut them down to size.

Bilqis left the sweeper muttering to himself. Not surprisingly, he got back to work. It was now time for breakfast. She asked Mumtaz to bring it out into the drawing room, where she liked to sit in the sunlight by the window. The girl brought out a tray with toast, a jar of Mitchell's marmalade and tea. The slices were arranged in a small wicker basket, under a thick cloth napkin, with a butter knife alongside it and another knife for spreading the marmalade.

Bilqis rustled open the newspaper. There had been clashes between police and protestors in the suburbs of Malir and Shah Faisal Colony. At least three people had been killed and eighteen wounded, raising the death toll in four days of rioting to eight. The troubles had begun when a Pathan bus driver, racing against another driver, ignored traffic lights, crashed into a car and then careered into a group of girl students from Sir Syed College in Liaqatabad. A Mohajir girl died of her injuries. When students from the college marched in protest, the police, in their usual heavy-handed way, charged them with batons. This attack on female students infuriated their male guardians. In the following days, Mohajir gangs rampaged on streets from Liaqatabad in the east to Orangi in the west, setting tires alight and torching buses that they thought belonged to the Pathans. In retaliation, a group of Pathans threw stones at a bus carrying Mohajir students to the girl's funeral, then invaded the campus of the nearby Abdullah Girls College, where they set the school's science laboratory on fire.

All of this would have meant little to Bilqis, but when Mumtaz's brothers were arrested by the police she had to become involved. Mumtaz's brothers drove minibuses. They claimed that they were picking up passengers outside Abdullah Girls College when the police pulled them out and dragged them away. The younger brother was badly beaten up and suffered from broken ribs. After they were in detention two days, Bilqis paid their bail for the sake of Hameeda, who was beside herself with worry. Fortunately, the police did not press charges, and the brothers were released.

When they came to thank Bilqis, she was touched by their gratitude. It was like having bodyguards. In a city where lawlessness was rising every day, she suddenly felt secure, but strangely tainted at the same time, because she did not know herself if the brothers were entirely innocent. Mumtaz's family were Pathans, and Pathans had become notorious in Karachi since the war in Afghanistan. There had always been Pathans in the city who lived amicably with the other communities, but the new ones pouring down from the Frontier province were a different breed altogether. They had taken over all the minibuses in the city, and they drove them recklessly, with complete disregard for the rules of traffic. Their mafia traded in smuggled goods, guns and narcotics. They even sold guns to their foes the Mohajirs, whom they had pushed out of the squatter colonies that they now inhabited. No one liked them, but the police and military did nothing to stop them and, since these agencies were dominated by Punjabis, the Pathans were regarded as their henchmen.

Bilqis put the newspaper away. Karachi used to be such a peaceful town. She remembered the time when the greatest threats to law and order were bicycle thieves. It seemed a world away from this city, where Mohajirs and Pathans, Punjabis and Sindhis, were at each other's necks. It was all General Zia's doing, she thought. He had pitted them against one another to gain mastery of them all. First he used the Pathans to break the influence of the Sindhis, but when the Pathans turned against him he started supporting the Mohajirs.

Pakistan was meant to be the Land of the Pure, a country where Muslims could live together, but faith was obviously not enough to unify the people. No sooner did they have a country than they developed grudges against one another, like the crowds in the Tower of Babel brawling in different tongues. She was reminded of Brueghel's *Tower of Babel,* with its ascending spiral and exquisitely drawn arches, reaching to the clouds. It had been her favorite painting ever since she was a girl. There was a magical quality of lightness and wonder about it, and she remembered how she used to pray that God would let her step into the painting and become part of it.

Bilqis smiled to herself as she recalled her happy childhood, which still radiated warmth and felt more immediate and real than the present. Her thoughts then returned to her grandchild. She felt a great need to see the baby, to smell her and touch her. If she could take the little thing into her care, then perhaps she could teach her something of the etiquette and manners that would make her less foreign. This thought, of evoking for the child something of the old world that was disappearing around her, lifted her spirits.

After finishing her breakfast, Bilqis retired to her study. A sheaf of exam papers lay piled on her desk. She opened the window. A breeze brushed the pages. Comforted by the assurance that at least the fate of her students lay in her hands, she soon became absorbed in her work. A few of the answers were mediocre and conventional, but the standard was surprising high. She marked every paper with care, writing out her comments in red ink in the margins. The scratch of the pen's nib, the flow of wet ink and the rustle of paper soothed her nerves. The world of letters was the best of all possible worlds, she thought. It was disinterested. It made no demands.

From time to time, her attention was drawn to an original remark that gave her pleasure, and then she changed her pens and put a little blue tick against it.

The kitchen screen door swung on its hinges, squeaked and slammed shut. The noise brought her down from her mystic spheres. It was old Hameeda. Bilqis could tell from the sound of her lopsided, shuffling gait. In she came.

"Well, Hameeda?" Bilqis remarked, looking over the rim of her glasses.

Hameeda sensed that her mistress had something to tell her. "What is it, begum sahiba?" she asked. "You seem to be in a good mood today."

"I have become a grandmother," Bilqis said, beaming.

"God be praised! Boy or girl?" Hameeda sat down on the carpet.

"Girl," Bilqis said, looking at her for a reaction. Hameeda was far too shrewd for Bilqis to see through her. She gave loud thanks to Allah and implored Him to keep the child in His safekeeping. It was as if she had had her response ready, a little too quick, too practiced to be genuine. The two women sparred and parried like this all the time. Bilqis let the matter pass. She watched as Hameeda produced a parcel from under her shawl: a bale of green georgette wrapped in yellow gift paper.

"What is this?"

"A sari piece for you," Hameeda said, offering it to her. "My brother-in-law brought it with him."

"Why would he bring me a sari piece?"

"Why wouldn't he, begum sahiba? You have done so much for us. It's the least he could do for you."

Bilqis scowled. A favor was usually asked for after an offering. She put down her pen. "There was really no need," she said coolly, as she unwrapped the package and examined the cloth. It was bright green and shiny, horrible. She could not wear it. Perhaps she could give it to the sweeper, making as if it were a gift from her. That way she would oblige him without any cost. She had to be as sly as they, she thought; otherwise they'd always get the better of her. Feeling a little better, she accepted with a murmur of thanks and waited for Hameeda to speak.

"As you know, begum sahiba, I have been wanting to marry off Mumtaz for a long time. I feared that we'd never find her a good husband. There were times when I sank into the deepest gloom. I lost all hope, but God has answered my prayers. May His wisdom be exalted."

"Who is it?"

"Mumtaz's uncle wants her to marry his eldest son."

"Your brother-in-law?" Bilqis looked at the sari piece.

"Yes, begum sahiba. God be praised. Our waiting days are over."

Bilqis was not a fool. She could very well see where this conversation was going. Long ago she had offered to pay for the girl's dowry, and now she was being asked to uphold her promise. She would pay for the dowry, and the girl would be traded like a heifer. Her manner turned glacial.

"What does Mumtaz think of it? Have you spoken to her?"

"She'll do what I tell her."

"I see."

"No, begum sahiba, you tell her," Hameeda implored, arms spread wide. "She listens to you. You tell her what she must do."

"Have you set a date?"

"Next year, God willing."

"A year will go fast," Bilqis said. "It all seems too rushed. She is too young. I don't know if this is the right thing for her."

"You know that's not true. She is a grown-up woman. She can't prance around the neighborhood anymore. She needs her own home.

It's time we found her a husband. You still have my younger daughter, you know."

Bilqis looked at the woman in glum silence. She had read her mind. "I can't think now, Hameeda," she said, arranging her papers. "I don't want to be late for my lectures. We will talk again."

"When?"

"When I have time."

After a meaningful pause, Hameeda rose. She went to the door, put on her rubber slippers and went out of the house. Bilqis was left alone but her peace was ruined. She had been expecting this conversation in the indefinite future, not today. Now it had happened, she found herself totally unprepared. Hameeda would be back another day. What would she say to her then? She would have to let go of Mumtaz. It was inevitable but the idea of letting go did not come to her easily. Mumtaz was one of a kind. Unlike most servants, she could cook and clean and do housework without any supervision. The girl had been with her since she was a child. Bilqis had seen her grow up in front of her eyes. She had spent more time with her than with her own son. Who could possibly replace her?

Bilqis's eyes were drawn to the oil portrait above the mantelpiece. A family heirloom in a heavy gold frame, it was the image of Hazrat Mahal Begum, wife and consort of Sultan Wajid Ali Shah, king of Oudh, who was related by marriage to Bilqis's great-great-grandfather Nawab Moeen-uddaula Bahadur. The handsome young woman had high cheekbones, a small chin and an aquiline nose. She was dressed in a bright orange gharara. An emerald-green dupatta embroidered with a gold edging covered her head. Her eyebrows were like crescent moons arched over deep black eyes. Bilqis looked at the portrait with admiration. A brave woman of indomitable will, she thought. What would she have to say about Bilqis's little troubles if she came back to life? The woman scowled down at her, passing judgment.

9

MUMTAZ RETURNED TO the house at noon. She unbolted the kitchen door and entered. The house was empty. Bilqis had left for the day and would not be back home until late afternoon. The girl breathed a sigh of relief.

She wiped the dining table and washed the dishes left over from the morning. After she had dried and put them in the cupboard, she mopped the floor, and mulled over whether she ought to dust the drawing room. Feeling lazy, she put away her cleaning things in the closet under the stairs and returned to the kitchen. She washed her hands, and rolled the dough, turning it into plump patties that she arranged in neat little rows on the white marble top. She hummed to herself but stopped after a while. She was unhappy. The thought of her wedding bothered her. She did not want to get married to her cousin. He was a dim, peripheral figure. She knew nothing about him except that he lived in faraway Attock, in a house that belonged to her forefathers. Her father had brought his family to Karachi while she was still very young. In all her life, she had seen this fellow only once or twice. She had not been asked if she wanted to marry him. She had been told, and she dared not refuse. The notion of making her own fate was quite unthinkable.

It was so often like this with her; thinking and doing were two very different things. She was biding her time now, waiting, hoping and praying for anything that might deliver her from her fate.

"I am to be married, yes, a fine thing it is, but what about love?" she muttered to herself. "My cousin wants to marry me because I am young and I will give him children, not because he loves me. Why should I marry him?"

She could have dwelt in the kitchen for the rest of the afternoon, musing and doing her chores, when she heard someone in the side lane. A cat was sitting on the wall outside the kitchen window, staring at her through the screen door.

"Mano?" she called out softly.

The cat's ears did not flicker.

Mumtaz loved animals. They understood and responded to her. It had been her idea to tame the cat. When the animal gazed at her with its green eyes, or licked her fingers with its sandpaper-like tongue, the tension in her body dissolved, even if the feeling was momentary. She went to the refrigerator and was about to put out a bowl of milk for the creature when she heard a faint knock at the kitchen door. A young man was standing there with a piece of paper in his hand. Mumtaz recognized him instantly. It was the chowkidar from the white villa across the road. She was surprised that he knew where to look for her. Then she remembered that she had left her slippers on the steps outside the side entrance. She turned around slightly.

"I brought you this." He held out an envelope.

"What is it?"

"It's a letter," he replied, averting his glance.

"Leave it on the table," she said.

"Over here?" He tentatively put it near the edge of a side table.

"Over there is fine."

The girl's fingers automatically scrubbed the bowl while her eyes remained settled on him. She had seen him only once or twice since Kate's visit. He had disappeared over summer and autumn and come back a few months ago, in the midst of winter. He had a clear, lean face with a fair complexion and dark brown hair. She thought that he would have passed for a Pathan except for his accent, which she could not place. He had dropped by a few times to run errands for Bilqis, but the two had never spoken. Sometimes they did not even glance at each other, as if the other person did not exist, but it was done with complete awareness.

"I think it's from the memsahib," he said.

"How do you know?"

"I know what you know," he said, smiling.

"It could be from anywhere."

"I read the address," he replied. "I'm educated, you know."

"Is that so?"

"Oh yes," he remarked, pleased. "I've been to college."

Mumtaz let out a little laugh. "If you've been to college then why are you a chowkidar? You should wear a shirt and tie and work in an office."

"I'm a security guard," he replied.

"It's the same thing."

"It's not the same thing. A security guard has power."

"Okay, in other words, you're a chowkidar of the better sort."

Omar's face turned red. His eyes gave away his age. He could not have been more than a few years older than she. Mumtaz thought that he looked handsome.

"Did you hear gunshots last night?" he said after a pause.

"The fireworks, you mean?"

"Those were not fireworks."

"You have a gun?"

He nodded. "A revolver," he said, regaining confidence. "I always keep it loaded. When I go to sleep, it stays under my pillow."

"Who were you firing at? Did someone break into the house?"

"I was firing at watermelons," he said solemnly.

"Why?"

"Target practice."

A smile flitted across the girl's lips. She glanced at him before turning back to her work. "My mistress says that you keep good watch," she said.

Omar seemed pleased. He leaned against the wall. His head cleared up a little and he looked at Mumtaz. She had a quick mind, he thought. Her playful manner was not how he expected a good girl to behave, but he found her humor appealing. She was very attractive.

"What else does she say?" he asked.

"I can't remember," Mumtaz said, frowning.

Omar moved inside the kitchen and stood with his hands behind his back. Next he leaned out of the doorway and peered into the dining room.

"May I have some water, please?"

There was something feline in his movements that Mumtaz liked. She poured him a glass of chilled water from the refrigerator.

"You have a poor memory," he said, returning the empty glass. "You should eat almonds. Eat them with milk before you go to bed and you'll have an elephant's memory. You'll never forget anything."

The girl's face softened. "I wasn't paying attention," she said, feeling charitable. "My begum could write you an endorsement. She knows everyone there is to know. One chit from her will get you a job anywhere you want."

"I don't want to ask for favors," he said, shaking his head.

"You're arrogant."

"I'm not arrogant. I know what sort of work is out there. I don't want it."

"You don't like to work?"

"You want to know the truth?"

The girl shrugged her shoulders.

"The truth is that I can find work. I am a trained electrician. I know the ins and outs of the trade. I can walk into any factory and they'd give me a job. I can make a lot of money if I want to, but I don't care for money. I'm not greedy. I don't want to live like that."

"Everyone else lives like that."

"But where's the honor in it? I need something greater and nobler than such life has to offer."

"What you do is not much better."

"Oh, this is just something on the side," he replied, not without a certain loftiness. "It's not what I really do."

"What *do* you do?"

His eyes shone. "You won't tell anyone else?"

She nodded, an accomplice.

"You must swear on something."

"I swear."

"Swear on your mother."

"I swear on my mother," Mumtaz said, trembling slightly. His eyes were running over her body.

"I'm a freedom fighter," he said.

Mumtaz had heard rumors from her brothers of young men who were going to fight in Kashmir against the Indians and Omar was one of them. She had not seen a freedom fighter in her life, but everything made sense now. She understood why he had refused her offer of help. It was what a bold, brave young man would have done.

For a while, they talked about nothing in particular. Omar asked her a great many questions about her family and her employer, Bilqis. He seemed interested in everything that she had to say. Then, out of the blue, he asked if she was alone in the house. Mumtaz had felt a peculiar happiness talking to him, but now she was offended.

"Is this how you talk to your sisters?" she snapped. "You ought to be ashamed."

"But you are not my sister," he said, smiling.

How dare he, she thought. "Well, perhaps you'd like my brothers to teach you a lesson," she said, glaring at him. "They'll put a knife between your ribs if you're not careful."

He burst out laughing. The tone surprised her. He sounded older and scornful, but her heart told her that he was not malicious. "I'm going to call you," he said, as he headed toward the door.

"You don't have the telephone number."

"Oh yes I do."

"But you won't dare."

"Oh yes I will."

"No!" Mumtaz shot back, but he had already left.

From that day, Mumtaz began waiting for the telephone to ring. Her mother and sister came to the house in the early morning and left around nine o'clock, after their chores were done. Once Bilqis went to the university, Mumtaz had the house to herself. She spent her time imagining how she would respond if Omar rang. Would she talk to him? Would she report him? What was the right thing to do? It was not like meeting someone face-to-face. He was just a voice on the other end of the line. She could make him disappear by hanging up. No one would ever know. Besides, she was not going to be instigating anything. If she did not encourage him, if she did not divulge anything to him, then she could do no harm. The more she thought about the risks, the more she wanted him to call.

Each day, Mumtaz stayed in the house until her mother fetched her in the evening. Never had she enjoyed her household chores as much—dusting, washing and mopping were duties that she discharged with a religious fervor, as if in the fulfillment of those duties lay the requital of all her hopes. Bilqis usually locked the rooms upstairs, where she left most of her valuables, but Mumtaz knew where she kept the keys and, to pass the idle hours, she fetched them and tidied up those rooms as well. She did not think about her wedding any longer and, even when that thought crossed her mind, it did not torment her like before. A week after her encounter with Omar, the telephone rang while she was dusting her mistress's bedroom. She flew down the stairs and leapt at the receiver, quite breathless as she picked it up. It was Kate wanting to talk to Bilqis. Mumtaz was so frustrated that she nearly burst into tears. It was the wrong time to be making conversation because Omar might be trying to call her. In the afternoon, the telephone rang again. She was there to pick it up.

"Hello?" she said softly.

There was a momentary silence. Then a male voice spoke. "Hello."

She slammed the telephone down. A few minutes later, it rang once more. "Hello!" This time, she reprimanded the caller, pretending she did not know who it was, and hung up, her heart beating fast. The next day Omar rang again.

She succumbed. The defenses came down one by one—from slamming down the telephone she became a mute listener before taking the first tentative steps of conversation. But like any education, even this process was achingly slow. For a long time, Omar could extract only halting monosyllables; it was later that she learned to giggle into the receiver without pretending reproaches.

Bit by bit, he told her about his life: elderly parents, a mother with chronic depression, a father with gout; two older brothers who owned a small pharmacy in Muzaffarabad, both with families; and a married sister living in Balakot. He was the youngest of the siblings. The family had been torn apart by the Partition. Two of his uncles lived on the Indian side of Kashmir. He remembered going down to the banks of the Neelum River with his parents as a child to see them gathered on the other side. The families used to shout at one another over the water and sometimes traded across baskets of fruit on a rope bridge. This was before the troubles began. No one went to the river anymore for fear of being shot.

One afternoon Omar told her how he joined the struggle when one of his uncles was killed by Indian soldiers who claimed he was a militant. "I couldn't go on living my life the same way after we found out what had happened. Some people can do it. They can hang their heads and reconcile themselves to misfortune, but there is a difference between misfortune, which is accidental, and injustice, which is deliberate, even if it is impersonal. I couldn't hang my head and pretend that everything was normal when it wasn't. Of course, my mother didn't want me to fight. She wanted me to stay. 'Stay for what?' I used to say to her. 'They shoot your brother and you want me to stay? They break our family apart and you want me to stay?' You can't draw a line through someone's house and say, 'Here's the border; half of the household will live on this side and half on the other and don't you dare cross this line because we will kill you if you do.' We are one people on this side and that side. If my people suffer on the other side, then I will go and fight for them. It's as simple as that. We didn't draw the Line of Control there. We didn't ask anyone else to put it there. What right does anyone have to impose it on us? It means nothing. I can stand on this side and piss on the other. That's what it means to me. You'll see. One day, by the grace of God, the whole of Kashmir will be ours. No one can deny us the land we belong to."

"What about your brothers? Did they take up arms too?" Mumtaz asked.

"They have children to take care of," Omar said. "They have no choice; I don't blame them; if I had children, I would not forsake them either, but I do have a choice. If I choose not to seek retribution, then I'm a coward."

"You must have broken your mother's heart."

He chuckled. "You're right. Mothers are such gentle creatures. They're always worried about what you eat and where you go and what you do. If mothers were running the world, everybody would be sitting at home. Cars and trains would come to a stop, planes wouldn't fly, ships wouldn't sail. Nothing would get done."

"They say you fought in Afghanistan," Mumtaz said.

"Who says?"

"People do. I heard my brothers say it."

"Well, it's true."

"Why were you fighting there?"

"Why not? It's a glorious cause," he said. "Nothing gives me as much pleasure as fighting for a cause. Without a cause, we're no better than animals. They live and die too. Tell me, what else did they say?"

"That you've killed Russians."

"Yes, of course, we killed lots of them. We gave them what they deserved. They invaded Afghanistan and look what happened to them. Afghanistan became their graveyard."

"One day you'll get killed for sure."

"It doesn't matter," he said. "I'm without fear. That's why I can fight."

Omar needed no encouragement to talk. His voice became animated as he told her how he trained at a camp where young Muslim volunteers were coming to fight the Russians from all over the world. He had met black Americans, Africans, Arabs and Bengalis. They understood one another because they knew what they were there for. Many of them could not even speak one another's language, but it did not matter. For six wonderful weeks they were like one big family. They prayed together, ate together and learned guerrilla tactics. They went into combat and were martyred. For each fallen comrade, a dozen young men came forward. The ranks of martyrs grew. No one was afraid to die. These men were his true brothers, he said.

The girl fell silent.

"Are you afraid for me?" he asked.

"Why would I be afraid for you?"

"Because you like me."

"I think you're presumptuous," Mumtaz replied. She could not permit such frankness, not yet, when she barely knew him, but there was something in her voice that told him that his trespass was not unwelcome.

They spoke to each other every day with a trust and lightness that flowed naturally between them. Omar would call her after the Zuhr prayers, and then they would talk for hours. The solitude, the empty house, the cawing of crows and the deep silence of those heady afternoons made them forget the passage of time. Every day, she went to the house feeling as if she were on the verge of a new adventure. Omar fascinated her with his stories of the battlefield: of eluding Russian helicopters in the valleys and ambushing armored convoys, of wading through icy rivers and hiding in caves. With loving detail he explained to her once how he learned to fire a rocket-propelled grenade launcher by picking off trees along a ridge until it looked like a freshly plowed field.

Sometimes he talked about his childhood, when he had believed in fairies and magic. "Don't think that I was always like this," he told her. "I had a cupboard full of fireworks. I used to make rockets that could shoot up into the sky like nothing you have seen. I was the best rocketeer in town. I'll tell you this—I wanted to be an astronaut. I wanted to fly to the stars. Then I grew up and I wanted to become a cricket player and a soldier, like all the other boys of my age, but my first memory is of wanting to be an astronaut."

In moments like these, Mumtaz wished for nothing except to listen to him speak. She had had little experience of the outside world, and his words had a strange effect on her. She listened to him with complete trust. He was very literate and ardent, confiding to her his deepest thoughts. Little by little, she saw her whole life reflected in his—whatever happened to her, her feelings, the thoughts that went through her mind, mattered only insofar as she was able to link them back to him. They were the only two people in the world, she felt, who understood each other.

Women had always been a mystery to Omar. In his childhood, he was told to venerate his mother. Paradise lay under her feet, went the saying, but in his youth he discovered that girls were not so divine. He had his first taste in Peshawar, where he lost his virginity to an Afghani girl. He had to pay her, but ever since this experience he found it difficult to accept that the Afghani girl and the women of his own family, his mother, sister and cousins, for example, were cast from the same flesh. What made some women wicked and others virtuous? Was it possible to seduce a virtuous woman? If a man seduced a woman, then didn't she have to be fundamentally wicked anyway? His feelings became even more turbulent when he started thinking about Mumtaz. Sometimes he longed to fuck her, and sometimes he thought about her soul and wondered if she was as lonely as he was. He liked hearing her voice. It soothed him. He liked the idea that the two of them were tied to each other by their thoughts. In a city where he knew no one except her, it made life bearable. One day, he rang her and asked if she had ever kissed a man.

"No, never," Mumtaz said.

"Will you kiss me?"

It was a daring advance, but Mumtaz didn't feel indignant. Her head spun with excitement. She cradled the receiver between her hands. "Do you have dirty thoughts on your mind all the time?" she asked. "What sort of Muslim are you?"

She was only half serious but his playfulness evaporated in an instant. "At least I pray, unlike you," he shot back, no longer joking. His tone became cold and harsh and, before she could say anything, he hung up.

10

A FORTNIGHT WENT by. Mumtaz was walking back from the bazaar late one afternoon. The sky was clearing after an early shower. The clouds were moving out toward the sea and the sun was descending in its arc, casting long shadows. Over a loudspeaker, a muezzin was calling the faithful to prayer. She covered her head with her shawl. An elderly man, holding up his trousers above his ankles, tiptoed over the puddles on his way to the mosque. She looked down to her left, where the ground fell away out toward what used to be the sea. A shanty town was fledging on the reclaimed land. In the diffuse sunlight, its dull metal roofs glowed like crustacean shells.

Mumtaz liked going to the bazaar. She would make her way from shop to shop, bargaining hard and not spending a paisa more than needed. She selected the produce with a proprietary air, and told the shopkeepers if their wares were not up to scratch. They all knew who she was. Many of them had known her since she was a scrawny child. They indulged her too, because she was pretty and plucky, and she livened up their day.

She walked with her grocery bags past the shrine of Abdullah Shah Ghazi, a Sufi saint who had lived and died in the eighth century. People came here from all over the city to make their wishes come true. Devotees were climbing up the small hill to the shrine. A fakir in patchwork robes held up the traffic as he stood in the middle of the road, whirling like a top. As cars edged past him, little beggar children dashed from the footpath and pressed their faces against the rolled-up windows. Later, they would share their spoils with the fakir.

Mumtaz liked this place. She liked the faint drumbeat of dhols coming from the hilltop, the cheerful sight of buntings hanging from trees. She liked drinking holy water from the well, which had burst forth at the feet of the holy man, who, perhaps irritated by the brackish water of the coast, had beseeched God for something more drinkable. These things gave the place an atmosphere of merriment. The occasional whiff of ganja only added to the general sense of anarchy that appealed to her.

The jacarandas blossomed. Beautiful gulmohar trees dripped with fleshy red flowers along the road. Invisible doves, drunk on the fragrance of jasmine, cooed to each other from their nests in the neem and peepul trees. A clutch of small boys raced past her on their bicycles, and then everything was quiet again. The road turned toward her neighborhood near the Clifton Pavilion. Soon she could see the pink spires of the Mohatta Palace through the treetops. She found herself wondering how she had never before seen the beauty of the things that she passed each day. Her head cleared, but not for long. Soon she was preoccupied with Omar's accusations. She could not understand how he called her faith weak just because she did not pray. It was hardly a crime. There were certainly things that she ought to do, just as there were things that he ought not to do. "God knows that I have my faith," she thought to herself. "I let my prayers slip, but I don't keep a false piety. I'm not a hypocrite. That God knows too."

While the invocation comforted her, she was struck by a new

thought. It was just possible that she had been reckless in challenging Omar's faith. Had someone doubted her morals because she was talking to him on the telephone, she would have been equally offended. Pride was a fragile thing. If only she hadn't opened that big mouth of hers, he would still be talking to her. What a silly girl she had been! He was right to be vexed with her. She scolded herself and started thinking of ways to make it up with him.

She stopped for a rest and shifted the load from one hand to the other; the bags were heavy, full of cauliflower, potatoes and a large green watermelon. She had not gone much farther when she heard the soft crunch of footsteps behind. She kept walking, and the footsteps continued. She thought it strange that a man would dare follow her in broad daylight. The alleys were never deserted. If anything happened, she could call out for help and there would be a dozen people pouncing on the fellow. She became more curious as he started making smacking sounds, as if blowing kisses. It was outrageous—she could not quite believe her ears. He was close now, singing a tune. When she was no longer in any doubt that the antics were meant for her, she stopped and turned around. It was Omar.

"Oh, it's you!" he exclaimed, feigning surprise.

"And who did you think it was?" she demanded, putting down her bags.

"I thought it was the Australian woman. I was singing a tune to cheer her up. Western women like singing and dancing."

"The Australian woman, ha!" she said, folding her arms. "You don't even know what she looks like."

"I do, of course. I saw her last year. When she was wearing the shalwar kameez, she looked just like you. You have the same height, the same hair and you're both so fair."

"Is that so?" Mumtaz rolled her eyes, picked up her bags and continued on her way. She was flattered, but she tried not to show it.

In a few moments, Omar leaped forward and was walking a few steps behind her.

"Why are you following me now?" She spoke in a low voice, without looking at him. She thought he was being rash.

"I'm not following you."

"Where are you going then?"

"Home, of course."

"I prefer walking alone," she said.

"I won't bother you. I just happen to be going the same way."

For a while, they walked in silence. When Omar started talking again, Mumtaz kept looking ahead, neither glancing at him nor giving him any sign. She feared that someone might see her with him and tell her mother, so she gave the impression that she did not care for him at all and there was nothing between them. In truth she gave him her full attention. They walked past an unsightly rubbish heap where a cat was scavenging with her kittens.

"Those stray cats don't stand much chance," he said.

"There are plenty of leftovers," she muttered, her lips barely moving.

"It's not the food," Omar said. "It's the pye-dogs."

"You're going to say something awful, aren't you? Don't tell me. I don't want to know."

Omar glanced at her. "Where did you find your cat?"

The girl shrugged. "What do you care?"

"Does she have a name?"

"Mano."

"That's a common name."

"Mano is a common cat."

Omar laughed. "One day Mano is going to dump a litter of kittens at your door."

"She already has. Would you take them?"

"Would I take them?" Omar echoed, raising his eyebrows at her. "I'd get rid of them for you."

"You won't keep them?"

"Cats are not loyal," he said. "I don't like them."

"But you won't drown them?"

"You say that as if I'm an ogre!"

Mumtaz gave him a cold look. "How should I know?" she said. "You're a man. Men can be ogres."

"I'll never harm you."

"What about other people?" she asked, blushing.

"I'll harm no man unless he is going to harm me."

"Then you're capable of harm."

"It goes with the territory," he said.

They walked in silence.

"Who gave you that black pashmina?" he asked.

"The begum sahiba did."

"Is it new?"

"I don't know."

"Why don't you tell the truth?"

"What do you mean?"

"That it's been handed down."

"What's that to you?"

"I could bring you bales of the real stuff."

"From Kashmir?"

Omar shrugged. "Where else? There's nowhere in the world where you can find pashmina as pure and soft as what I can bring you. That's my promise."

"And what if I find something better?"

"Then you can rub my face in dirt."

They exchanged a glance. Mumtaz knew that he was pleased with what he saw in her eyes. They reached the cul-de-sac where they lived. The sun had set and the light was fading. They heard a faint meow and saw Mano trot out through gate. She came to where Mumtaz stood and rubbed against her leg. A moment later, one of her scrawny kittens followed, floundering and keeling over like a half-drowned rat. Mumtaz knelt and picked up the small animal. Its body shuddered like a small motor as it purred. They looked at its pointy ears. For a moment, there was something childlike about them as they stood together absorbed in playing with the creature, and yet they were old enough to know that it was only the pretense of play. Nearing voices pulled them up.

"We've spoken on the telephone for long enough," Omar said softly. "Let's meet sometime."

"Impossible," Mumtaz murmured.

"Everything is possible," Omar said, his face near hers. "I want to take you to a circus."

"You're a scoundrel."

"But you like that, don't you? You like the scoundrel in me."

"Go now!" Mumtaz hissed. "If my mother sees me talking to you, she'll throttle me."

11

ON FRIDAY OF the following week, after clearing away the lunch plates, Mumtaz hurried off to meet Omar. Bilqis had come home early, as it was a half-day and lectures finished before the Jumma prayers. Mumtaz served her lunch as usual and waited for her to retire upstairs for her nap. When she was certain that Bilqis had fallen asleep, she sneaked out of the kitchen door and walked the hundred yards down the street to Clifton Road.

She had planned the adventure on the phone with Omar, but now that she was actually doing it, she felt frightened. Her heart pounded in her chest. The hair at the back of her neck stood on end. If anyone was going to catch her sneaking away, it would be on this stretch. At any moment, she expected a shout—her mother, one of her brothers, her father, even Bilqis herself—summoning her back, asking her where she was going and why. In spite of all these fears, she was full of courage. How pleasant it was to turn her back to duty. How pleasant not to linger in the kitchen at someone's beck and call. Her strength grew with every step. She could think of numerous excuses if anyone noticed her absence. She could tell Bilqis that her mother had sent her on an errand, and she could tell Hameeda that Bilqis sent her. No one would know otherwise unless they checked the facts with each other. And they had no reason to do so.

As she neared the end of the street, she started walking faster. She glanced over her shoulder and saw the house's gate in the distance. The street was empty. She broke into a run as she turned the corner, and then she was out of sight. The invisible tether had failed to pull her back. Nothing was insurmountable now. She looked to her right where Omar was waiting under the shade of a tree. He gave her a nod. She covered her head with her shawl and went to stand beside him. His eyes were focused intently on the passing traffic. Without exchanging a word with her, he hailed a rickshaw. They climbed in and the rickshaw drove off.

Although the backseat was cramped, the two sat slightly apart. So free and easy with each other over the telephone, they became tense in each other's company. Omar looked at her warmly but he did not quite know what to say. Mumtaz lowered her eyes when he talked. After a few mundane remarks, he fell silent. Mumtaz sat mute and frozen and stared out of the open window. After the euphoria of her escape, she was gripped by anxiety. She tried to reason and tell herself that all she was doing was going to the circus, but of course it wasn't just a matter of an outing. She was an unmarried girl going out with a man she barely knew. It was the wrong thing to do and she knew that very well. She was letting down her people, she felt. She was violating the trust of her mistress. She feared discovery and censure, and she veered between defiance and shame.

Twenty minutes later, they were standing outside the gate of the Lucky Irani Circus. The Lucky Irani was the only touring circus of the grand tradition that had survived. Its visit had been announced in newspaper advertisements, featuring lions, clowns and acrobats. The organizers had put up their tents on vacant ground on Newman Road and were hosting three shows daily, at eleven in the morning, three in the afternoon and, the most popular, six in the evening. Omar had persuaded Mumtaz to come with him to the afternoon show, which finished in time for her to return to the house just before she was expected.

A large billboard hung above the gate, but the cheap rendering made it look like a film poster. The artist had given the lions human-like faces, which made them appear quizzical rather than fearsome. A raging gorilla with bloodred lips looked as if he had mistakenly chewed on betel leaf and cardamom. His howling expression and chest thumping seemed like a gesture of lament.

There were two ticket booths, one for men and the other for women. There was a long queue on the men's side. It was actually more of a throng than a queue and, despite the efforts of the circus organizers to contain it, the crowd threatened to spill over into the women's section. A few impatient youths had already jumped the rail and were demanding tickets from the clerk in the women's booth. Surveying the situation, Omar dispatched Mumtaz to purchase the tickets while he waited at a distance. The youths shrank away as Mumtaz appeared. They watched her with blank expressions and fell back upon the booth again once she left with Omar.

A chained elephant stared down at the pair as they walked among the attractions. There were some families, but most of the visitors were male. The few couples they saw were newlyweds, who could be spotted easily because they were dressed up and bashful with each other. Children with kohl eyes wandered around licking on big sticks of cotton candy. A posse of midget wrestlers hurried by, following a fat woman with a tail. People loitered about a stall to shoot air pellets at balloons, but even at fifteen feet they missed because the wizened stallkeeper had heated the metal barrel of his gun over a flame to curve its trajectory. Next to the main pavilion, a daredevil motorcyclist drove fast inside a Wall of Death.

Everyone seemed to be having a good time. Even the amateur

marksmen looked pleased when they adjusted their aim to compensate for their deviant pellets. Mumtaz, however, watched everything with the wary eyes of an escaped convict. Talking on the telephone had been a game, a little fun that harmed no one, but behind the voice there was a real person, and being with him was very different from hearing his voice.

She walked around with Omar, hoping that people took them for husband and wife, but in her tortured imagination, everyone around her knew that she was a fake. The entire setup was a portent: the children, the families, the newlyweds, the marksmen whose shots were going astray—they all were placed there by a higher authority to remind her of her wickedness. All the circus curiosities turned monstrous, and became divine instruments of punishment. In her mind, she was trampled by an elephant, hurled by her hair and thrown into an arena of hungry lions, impaled on a wheel and pierced by daggers. The sensation became even more acute when the couple entered a candy-striped pavilion. In the collection of freaks gathered here from all over the world, she saw a metaphor of her own loathsome self.

The mermaid did not appear as the fey, magical creature of legend, but as a lecherous temptress of the underworld who had risen to bid her welcome. She was sitting in a kiosk on a platform of artificial coral. She wore a pink blouse and matching pink scales, but the idle way with which she combed her hair and flapped her fishtail showed the mannerisms of a harlot. The snake-woman appeared equally brazen as she sat coiled on a dais. She was beautiful, with dark eyes, arching eyebrows and black hair cascading upon her shoulders, but when she hissed she revealed a long, lizardlike tongue. Everything seemed cursed. In the laboratory of a mad scientist, Mumtaz stared at a severed head propped up on a chopping block. Blood oozed from its decapitated neck, but the eyes were alive. They rolled in their sockets and darted left and right. When they found Mumtaz staring at them, they stared back, as if saying, "I chose my own fate. I rejoiced in the flesh. Now I live the half-life of the damned! Go and take your pleasure too. Go and do what you please, but behold the punishment that awaits you."

Omar understood the look of despair on Mumtaz's face and felt responsible. Too far gone now, he kept up a brave pretense. "Come, come, there's a perfectly whole man sitting under that table. It's just a trick," he said out loud, as if he were comforting a frightened spouse, and ushered her toward the last kiosk, where they faced a two-headed gorilla. As the people streamed out of the pavilion, someone shouted: "The gorilla is out of the cage—he is free!" They heard the creature roar, pound its rubber chest and break open its cage. Then another cry: "The gorilla has just wrung a man's neck— run for your lives!" It was someone's idea of a prank. There was panic. Mothers herded screaming children, hobbling old men and young couples, amused and alarmed, retreated to the exit and bunched up in a thick mass while rogues grabbed at passing women, adding to the pandemonium.

In the excitement, Mumtaz realized that Omar had clasped her hand. Her hand went limp in his; moments later he let it go and, magically, something changed inside her. The very things that had terrified her now consoled her. Here amid the jostling crowd the two of them could walk like human beings. No one gave them a second glance. No one cared. They were like everyone else. The indifference of life struck her as beautiful, and she let go of her worries.

When Omar saw her smiling, he became cheerful too. In the main pavilion, they clapped their hands at trapeze artists. A clown entered the ring, followed by a bear in hot pursuit. They laughed at the spectacle as they sat side by side, their knees touching. Amid the sound of drums, they watched the ringmaster in red livery announce the finale. He was an ancient-looking man, as behooved a ringmaster, gaunt and straight-backed, and boasted a formidable mustache.

"Ladies and gentlemen! Boys and girls! This is the moment you have been waiting for! This is what it is all about! In all the lands near and far, of all the wonders great and small, the Lucky Irani Circus presents the greatest wonder of them all. Sit down! Be still! Be silent! From farthest Africa, we bring you four monarchs—they are the kings of the jungle, ladies and gentlemen, the lords of all beasts! Behold the lions of the Kalahari!"

A female lion tamer sauntered into the arena carrying a whip. She was a blonde in a red leather jumpsuit and cowboy boots. She came to stand in the middle of the arena and blew on a whistle. Then she clapped her hands. Four lions entered. They went around the arena once; she cracked her whip—they trotted along faster and, at a sign from her, climbed up on their stools, roaring like grouchy monarchs, except that, like the rest of the circus, there was something a little faded about them. They were old and their fur was coarse and shaggy, but the show had such spirit that no one seemed to mind.

The lion tamer walked past one of her charges and brushed its whiskers with the back of her hand. The lion made a purring noise and swiped at her gently with its paw. Next a lackey brought out an iron hoop wrapped with cotton wool.

The lion tamer doused it with gasoline and set it alight, using the flame to light a cigarette afterward. For a moment she surveyed the audience, holding her cigarette like a film star. Then, cracking her whip, she made the lions jump through the flaming hoop one after the other. She set another hoop on fire and the lions leaped in turn through two rings. When the show finished, she stamped out her cigarette with her heel and bowed to the audience. The speakers blared out the national anthem and everyone stood up. Even the lions rose on their hind legs until the recording came to its scratchy end.

After the circus, Omar and Mumtaz loitered outside the tents. As it grew dark, the vendors lit gas lamps and charcoal braziers. The entire encampment, with its stalls, marquees and myriad booths, glittered like a small township. They went aimlessly from one stall to another, neither one in any hurry to go home. Mumtaz was now rapt with the outing. The sound of a bear snorting as a dwarf led it past them, the hubbub of the crowd, the aroma of food—all reminded her of the fairs she used to go to as a child. They sat down by an ice cream stall to eat faluda.

"I always wanted to see the lions. They're so perfect," Omar said.

"You did not despise the whole thing?"

"Why should I despise it?"

"You did not mind the woman?"

"She was Iranian," Omar replied placidly, as if that explained everything.

"She looked like a Westerner to me," Mumtaz said.

"No, she had dyed her hair. I'm sure of it. That's what a lot of Iranians were like when the Shah was in power. They thought that copying Europeans and Americans was progress, eating pig meat was progress, dancing and drinking and dyeing their hair blond was progress. And look what's happening in Iran now. The wrath of God has fallen upon them."

Omar became garrulous after eating his portion, and spoke excitedly about his favorite topic, the liberation of Kashmir. Just as other nations had won independence, he explained, there was no reason why their own struggle could not end in victory. All they needed was the nerve to fight. He was full of ideas, and he spoke with an independent air that stirred her admiration. He said that while he was not a violent man, there were times when violence was justified.

"There is good and there is evil," he said. "Evil is like the devil and it comes in many forms. It's not just people who are evil. Laws may be evil. Governments may be evil. Things that are legitimate and respectable may be evil. God gave us our intellect so we may distinguish good from evil. It's a Muslim's duty to fight evil in whatever form it exists."

He was frowning, but a strange, fierce smile spread across his face as he looked at her.

"I've seen the bottles of water you keep in that refrigerator," he said. "Do you know what they are? Old whiskey bottles."

"They belong to the sahibs," Mumtaz said, meaning Hashmat and Sikander.

"I knew it," Omar said. "Alcohol is forbidden in Islam, yet your masters drink. They make merry while you and I sit here like dogs. They call themselves Muslim, but they're worse than infidels. They're apostates and hypocrites. They'll burn in the nether regions of hell."

"They are nice people," Mumtaz said. "They've always done the right thing by me. What they do in private is not my concern. I cannot judge them for that."

Omar's eyes shone. "Of course not all rich people are bad. Not all aristocrats are bad. There are always nice people among them. I'm sure that your mistress is nice too. I certainly don't hold a grudge against her, but it's the class she represents that's bad. Tell me, do you have to wash their dishes and tidy their beds?"

"Yes."

"And do you eat after they've eaten?"

"Yes."

"That proves my point. They're nice enough to give you left-overs, but you're still their servant. That's the problem with you—I mean with you and me and all the rest of us. We get a pat on our head and a full belly and we go away wagging our tails. As long as there are rich folk, they will look down upon us poor folk. They'll have the pick of everything while we live on their crumbs. Isn't that so? What is our fault except that we are born poor? All men are equal before God, so why is it that we are less equal than they? I'm educated, so why is it that I have to work for them? I'll tell you why. They want to keep us down. They want to keep us down because they are incapable of even lifting a finger themselves. But why should we serve them? It's about time we shook them up."

Omar's tenderness disappeared when he spoke about things he disliked. When he became passionate, he turned into another person altogether. Mumtaz did not like him talking about Bilqis in that tone. She was her employer, but her house was Mumtaz's home too. She had grown up there. She couldn't just turn around and start bad-mouthing her mistress. A burning anger overcame her. For the first time since meeting him, she judged him, so upright, so pious, fighting for a cause, talking about the Almighty, but with the same mouth, demanding kisses from her and pouring scorn on everyone else. Fraud, hypocrite! What a fool she had been to see the world through his eyes!

"I should be going home," she said as she folded her arms, adjusted her shawl and rose to leave. She went to stand by the roadside and watched the traffic go past. When a rickshaw slowed down, she hailed it and slipped inside. Omar watched her get in but she avoided his glance. The pair of eyebrows and eyelashes painted over the rickshaw's headlights gazed at him like a pair of houri eyes, reflecting his own dispassionate stare. A bemused smile spread across his face.

"Deep inside, you know that I tell the truth," he said. "If someone were to kick out your mistress and give you the keys to her house, saying, 'Go! You are free! Sit in their chairs, eat from their plates, sleep in their beds! Go!' you wouldn't take her place. You'd wait for someone else to give you orders. I know. You serve them and that makes you think that you're one of them. You sympathize with them, don't you? You don't even know that you are a servant.

You should be careful that you don't become too refined. One day you may even look down on me." He was shouting when he finished.

"To hell with you," Mumtaz shouted back.

When the vehicle swung around, he caught sight of the painting on its rear. Between the dim red taillights, a winged horse with a woman's head rose from a moonlit valley toward paradise.

12

BILQIS SAT ON her bed and thought about what she needed to pack. On her bedroom floor lay a pair of dusty suitcases, one large and black and the smaller one red, both with old clothes stored in them. Bilqis had not opened them in years. Mumtaz had brought them down from the attic for her trip, and laid them out on the floor, sensibly spreading old newspaper underneath to prevent the carpet from getting dirty. Everything was organized except for her packing. The flight was booked, the university had been informed, the newspaper subscription canceled. The house was to be left in the servants' care. Hameeda's husband and her sons were to take turns sleeping on the veranda. Bilqis was going to lock up the upstairs section, as she did not like the idea of the servants, especially their menfolk and children, swarming around the television or peeking into her bedroom. The downstairs section would remain unlocked, as they were allowed to use the kitchen and keep their food in the refrigerator. They could also take incoming calls, but a small brass padlock on the telephone prevented them from making calls. Bilqis had learned from experience that this arrangement of limited privileges worked best. Any more and she risked excesses, and any less, neglect.

It was summer. The birds chirped outside and the sun shone bright. Bilqis started to cough. She had persuaded the doctor that she was well enough to travel, but she felt that something was not quite right. Little beads of perspiration appeared on her brow. Her son had become a father, but her own loneliness was increasing. She wasn't meant to be catching a flight to see her grandchild. That's not how things were supposed to be. Her grandchild and her family were meant to be here. They should have been visiting her, not the other way around. That's what had made her ill. Her life was in discord with the natural order of things. Living alone was not easy. That wasn't how families were supposed to live, disconnected from one another. It wasn't even how her servants lived.

"Distances are shrinking," Mahbano would tell her over the telephone. "You can get on a plane and be in Lahore in an hour. You can fly to Melbourne and see Samad tomorrow. And what am I here for? All you have to do is call me and we can talk for as long as you like."

Sometimes Bilqis wished she had her sister's optimism. Mahbano was so rational, so confident, but then she had her husband. She could draw strength from him. Bilqis had no one. The servants obeyed her and were loyal to her, but she had to keep a certain distance. She couldn't confide in them. She couldn't share her emotions with them, or her fears. If she lowered herself to their level and tried to become their friend, she would lose their respect.

Bilqis undid the latches on the black suitcase and lifted its lid. It was like opening a time capsule. The clothes lay in neat layers, as if each layer represented an epoch, or period of life that she could turn over to excavate deeper and deeper into her past. Saris too bright to wear at her age, shawls no longer her favorites, a brown tweed coat, trousers and shirts that had belonged to her husband—everything was there. Hashmat's clothes had always smelled of an English cologne of lime extract that his friends used to bring back for him from Jermyn Street in London. Its scent was gone now. The smell of naphthalene had long ago replaced it. She ran her fingers along the rim of the suitcase to find other mementos: old fountain pens, a photo album, a diary. She had packed the suitcase herself after Hashmat's funeral and, as she knelt down to examine its contents, the memories returned.

Bilqis was struck by the presentiment of disaster the night Hashmat had died. Samad was studying overseas. She and Hashmat were alone in the house. When they sat down for dinner, he told her that he did not like what was happening in the country. It was all right now but in ten years, in twenty years, it was going to be a very different place. The Islamization, the gradual descent into medievalism, was not to his taste. In fact, he had grave misgivings about it, but his despondent talk was nothing new. He had been deeply unhappy ever since General Zia and his cabal had overthrown Zulfiqar Ali Bhutto. Hashmat was fond of Bhutto. They were both old Oxonians, Westernized and secular men. The military and the Islamists were in cahoots against them. That he understood. He knew that Bhutto was not without faults, but he was the best of a bad lot. He was a demagogue, yes, but he gave people hope. After him, there were only mullahs and generals. Once Bhutto fell, there were big troubles ahead for people of his class. That he knew too.

They would hang Bhutto, he told her. They would convict him of a crime, pervert the truth and hang him.

"He is too popular to be hanged," Bilqis said.

"That is precisely why they will hang him."

"And make him a martyr?"

"Have you ever seen a dead man hold a rally? Who will lead the people? They will be quite headless, I assure you."

Bilqis resented his scornful tone. She did not like the way Hashmat dismissed her sometimes, as if her thoughts and opinions were of no account. Why couldn't he let her speak without making her feel ridiculous? She too liked Bhutto. She too cared what happened to him. Was she not entitled to voice her feelings? They did not speak to each other again for the rest of the evening.

The memory, with all its emotions, was frozen in her recollection. She heard him wake up in the middle of the night, just as he used to. After waking up, he burped. She sleepily turned on her side to face him and saw his back in the gloom. He had put on his brown sleeping gown with tassels and was sitting on the edge of the bed. She heard him mumble something. Then she heard him tear open the wrapping of a Gelusil tablet and reach for his glass. He was suffering from his usual indigestion, she thought. She closed her eyes and heard him rise and shuffle toward the bathroom, where the lightbulb had gone out. The flip-flop of his rubber slippers on the concrete floor, the crickets singing outside the window, were familiar and mundane sounds. She heard him urinate, flush the toilet, clear his throat, spit, turn on the tap—and then she heard him fall. For a moment, she did not recognize the thud of a human body hitting the tiles. She thought that he had slipped on a patch of water. In the split-second silence that followed, she knew that something worse had happened.

Heart disease was hereditary in his family. The year before he had complained of chest pains on his regular walks. The heart specialist at Mideast Hospital told him that his cholesterol was high and the coronary artery on the left side of his heart was totally blocked. He was put on a diet of garlic capsules and statin drugs. All rich and heavy foods were prohibited. The specialist recommended angioplasty, but his friends warned him not to put too much faith in Karachi doctors. God knew they were all upstarts and pretenders. They urged him to go to London for a bypass operation at Cromwell or St. George's, but Hashmat was put off by the idea of surgery. Then there was the matter of obtaining visas from the British Consulate and the humiliating ordeal of convincing the consular official—an ordinary clerk who carried on like a viceroy—that they were not intending to stay illegally after their visas expired. In the weeks and months of procrastination that followed, the couple decided instead to go to Murree.

The great charm of Murree was that the place brought one to stillness. It took a few days for the effect to occur, but the sensation was inescapable. The passage of time had an indolent quality about it or, perhaps, as there was nothing to do, one was spared the remorse for time lost. The cool air, the thrill of being in a new place, the long, meandering walks overlooking valleys where scattered metal roofs of houses glinted here and there on the wooded slopes, delighted the couple. It was like a second honeymoon, but for months after Hashmat's death Bilqis wondered if the trip had been reckless. He died at home in Karachi, but she could not help thinking that the strain of travel and the thin air at high altitude had precipitated the chain of events. Had they not gone, he might have lived. Had she called the ambulance earlier, the extra minutes might have saved his life.

Bilqis wondered what those last muttered words were. What did he say with his back to her? Survivors of heart attacks report that it begins with shortness of breath and a heavy pain in the arms. Was he trying to tell her something? He knew the warning signs, so why didn't he call out to her? And why was she not more vigilant? Why did she not ask him if something was wrong? Was she still feeling miffed by the way he had spoken to her at the dinner table? Was that what had kept her from saving him? All the ifs and buts of the past taunted her with illusions of what her life might have been. And once these weak and foolish thoughts started, it was a slippery slope to darkness. The days that followed his death were all the same, repetitive and familiar. It was as if her thoughts had come to inhabit the house, like spirits, and she was unable to cast them out.

When the chancellor invited her to become a guest lecturer on literature at the University of Karachi, she was relieved to accept but suffered from seeing the decay in literary standards, which she associated with the decline of her own fortunes. She disliked campus politics and, aside from teaching, avoided university life as much as possible. Life went on. Her acquaintances told her how much they admired her fortitude; adversity had made her stronger, they said; in her place, they couldn't have coped at all; but Bilqis was numb to their praises. Behind her back, these same people had very different things to say. Hameeda volunteered the gossip she heard from other servants who eavesdropped on their employers' conversations. She was a good spy and reported everything without being asked.

"Begum sahiba, a pox on them! That is what I have to say," Hameeda told her one day. "I may be old and foolish, but these ears of mine, they hear everything and what they hear is terrible! There are people saying that the begum has lost her mind! That she has thrown away nothing that the master, may God rest his soul, possessed. They say his clothes are still hanging on the rack in his wardrobe, pressed and washed; his books are still on their shelves, although the sun has turned the pages yellow. May I be spared, but it is also rumored that even his reading glasses lie on the mantelpiece, within easy reach—for what, should he ever return? Lies, all lies! As God is my witness, I swear upon my head that they have not come from me. We may be poor and wretched, but we are not informers. We don't go about telling others what goes on in our house. May God punish those who are guilty. Oh woe!"

She slapped her forehead and went on. "When the sahib was alive, no one dared cross the line. Their mouths were shut because, if anyone said anything foolish, the sahib put them in their place.

They used to come to him with heads bowed and hands raised in supplication. And now look how the same people blabber on."

Bilqis was fond of her servant because she felt everything Bilqis felt, except she felt it more acutely because her pride was more touchy, her pain deeper. What if she turned things into a matter of personal honor? What if she thundered or wept about matters beyond her jurisdiction? At least she was loyal, thought Bilqis. Loyalty accounted for a great deal and made up for most things, but she wasn't quite sure if it gave Hameeda the right to feel pity.

"Those times are gone, Hameeda," she said resentfully. "Gone! What use is it crying over spilled milk? One never achieves anything by dwelling in the past, does one?"

13

IT WAS SEVEN o'clock in the evening in Melbourne, the end of a wintry day. Bilqis was sitting down for dinner at Samad's house in the beachside suburb of Hampton. The long red-gum table was set for three. The dining room was spacious and warm, with a slate floor and white walls. A log fire burned in the fireplace. A large window looked out into a garden full of lavender bushes, birds-of-paradise flowers and phormiums. Bilqis could see the gray silhouette of plants and the level black grass. The sun had set and it was dark, but the sky was clear and Venus shone bright. It never ceased to amaze her how clear the night sky was in Melbourne. Only when she was a child in Darjeeling could she remember seeing the Milky Way shimmer like it did here.

Samad laid out the table and Kate brought the food from the kitchen. She had made gnocchi with a tomato sauce and shaved parmesan, oven-baked garlic bread and salad. She dimmed the lights, lit a candle and sat down opposite Samad. Bilqis sat between them at the table head. Everyone spoke in low voices. The baby was asleep next door in her room. From time to time, Tara roused and Kate went in to check on her. Bilqis followed, unable to resist the temptation of seeing the peaceful face of the sleeping child. She had been delighted that the baby had come into her arms naturally, as if she had known her grandmother all along. In the photographs that Samad had sent her in Karachi, Tara seemed chubby with scant hair, and looked as pale as boiled cabbage. The forehead was a little broad, the nose a little too snub. There was ample likeness to her mother's side but little to her father's. Bilqis had fancied a more dainty child, but it was a quibble. As soon as she saw the baby for the first time and held her, she fell in love with her. The mouth and chin were delicately formed, and her skin was like porcelain, wonderfully translucent. Bilqis was convinced that she would become a beautiful woman.

Conversation turned to the weather. Kate started telling her mother-in-law how they had not had a decent summer this year. She did not swim in the sea even once. Samad said that he would never get used to the weather. He frequently suffered from colds, although he was usually able to shake them off in a matter of days. He had learned to keep a supply of vitamins at hand. Every time he felt the first symptoms of a cold, he doubled his dosage. Bilqis did not object to vitamins—she placed great faith in all medication—but she did not like Samad's diet, which seemed to consist of pasta, potatoes and meat.

"You should eat more fruit," Bilqis said.

"I have an apple a day."

"Do you take the skin off?"

"I wash it."

"With soap?"

"No, I don't have time for that. I wash it under the tap."

"You have to be very careful about pesticides."

"Fruit takes too long to prepare," Samad said, looking at Kate. "It has to be peeled and cut and it makes my fingers sticky. I'll eat it if someone peels it for me."

"You have hands, don't you?" Kate said teasingly.

"I've got better things to do with them."

Bilqis looked on as Kate and Samad bantered. An indulgent smile appeared at the corner of her lips. She was pleased for them, but she felt betrayed at the same time. Kate had won Samad from her. She had got everything without conceding anything in return. How was that possible? How had she earned that right? Love, yes, she loved Samad, but did hugs and kisses constitute love? Did murmuring "I love you" constitute love? What good was such love when the house hadn't been cleaned, the dishes weren't washed or the laundry hadn't been hung up to dry?

"What's the gnocchi like, Mother?" Samad asked. "Don't you like it?"

"It's soft," Bilqis said pleasantly. She poked at the pasta with her fork. After several weeks of subsisting on Western cuisine, she missed her own food. "One day, I'd like to cook a nice biryani for you," she said.

"We'll need to get the ingredients," Samad said.

"Are there any Indian shops around here?"

"Not for miles."

"Where do other Pakistanis buy their groceries?"

"I have no idea."

"Don't you know any Pakistanis?"

"None," Samad said coolly.

"Why?" Bilqis seemed surprised. "Aren't there any here?"

"There are a few, but I steer clear of them."

"What's wrong with them?"

"There's nothing wrong with them. They're just not my type."

"They're still your people," Bilqis said.

"That doesn't mean I have to be friends with them. All they care about is how much I earn and if I'm a good Muslim or not. That's not the sort of people I want to be friends with."

"I knew a Pakistani woman where I was working," Kate said.

"Was she a lawyer?" Bilqis asked.

"Yes. I thought she was from Turkey until she told me that her family was from Pakistan. We used to go out for lunch and have long chats, but we lost touch after she had her first child. She stopped working, like myself."

"Do you miss your work?"

"Sometimes," Kate said. "Samad thinks that I sit around all day and have cups of tea."

"When did I say that?" Samad protested.

"I'm only joking," Kate said. "Samad is good, actually. He knows what it's like. I don't have any time for myself. When Tara is awake, she needs my constant attention. I have to feed her. I have to clean her. I have to put clothes on her and hold her. I'm not saying that I don't like it—I love being a mother—but I envy my friends who don't have babies or who manage to juggle their careers and families. They contribute to society. What do I do? Sometimes I'd like to be like them and go back to work, but who is going to look after Tara? My parents can't look after her all the time."

"Can't you work part-time?" Bilqis asked.

"There's no such thing as part-time work in law. You either work full-time and bill all hours or you don't work at all. If we had more women partners, it would be different, but women don't stay in law because it's the men who set the rules. They make life hard for us."

"If you were in Pakistan, Mumtaz could look after her," Bilqis said. "She could be the nanny. I've seen her look after her little nephew."

Kate shook her head. "You know that I can't live in Pakistan, Mrs. Khan," she said. "My home is here. My family is here. This is where I belong."

Samad looked at both women as a chill descended. He wiped his lips with a paper napkin and pushed his plate to one side. Why did Kate have to answer Bilqis's remark literally when it was only a rhetorical comment? Why did she have to be so serious about something that was so abstract? And his curmudgeon of a mother—how could he have her on his conscience when she became infirm? Or did she want him to suffer, in revenge, for the moral responsibility that, in her mind, he had for her?

A few nights ago Bilqis had awoken with a severe pain in her lower back. The sensation went away in the morning, but if she had to stand for a while or walk a distance, the irritation began anew. Samad took her to the doctor, where an X-ray confirmed hip damage. Along the edges of her hip joints, the doctor showed her the traces of wear and tear on her hip joint, a fairly common condition at her age. He advised her to sleep on a flat, thin mattress. The deterioration had been quite dramatic since last year, when she had experienced no such trouble at all. She was told to do exercises and walk a little every day, even if it was somewhat painful. Samad could not help thinking what might happen if she fell seriously sick and he could not be by her side.

"It's time you came to live here, Mother," he said, breaking the silence at the dinner table. "You can't stay in Karachi forever."

Bilqis gave him a long, hard look. "Where would I live?" she asked.

"We'll find you a flat."

"A flat?" She laughed bitterly. "Why would I trade my house and servants for a flat?"

"You're not getting any younger, Mother," he said. "I know that you trust your servants, but when they realize how much you depend on them they'll take advantage of you. They're not family."

"They're the closest thing I have to a family," Bilqis said. She had been talking in English for Kate's benefit but now she spoke in Urdu.

Another long, despondent silence followed. "I know that I haven't done everything that you wanted me to do," Samad said, also turning to Urdu, "but I cannot undo what I have done."

"I don't expect you to," Bilqis answered. There was a strange pleasure in hearing what seemed like repentance. Neither of them looked at Kate.

"Then what do you want from me?" Samad asked.

"Nothing."

"Nothing?"

"All right, I want you to say that you'd do anything for me. I want to know that if I ever asked you for something, whatever it might be, you'd do it without question, without resenting me, that's all."

"I can't go back—you know that," Samad said. "I've settled here. I have a house here, a wife here. My work is here. When Tara grows up, she's going to go to school here. I can't just give up every-thing and head back home one day if you ask me to."

"You set your own limits, Samad."

"I just want to be honest, Mother. I don't like us having these vague, nebulous expectations from each other. It does us no good."

"My coming here isn't going to solve anything."

"Why not?"

"I am not a canary in a cage. You can't just bring me here be-cause it placates your conscience."

Kate looked on as the two argued. She did not understand what they were saying to each other, but she understood the angry tone of their voices. They were probably arguing about where Bilqis ought to live, but they could just as well be arguing about her, in front of her and in her own house, as if she had no right to it. She told herself that they had become oblivious of her, and that it did not matter because it was only natural for them to talk in their own language, but she had never imagined how easily and swiftly they could bar her from things that were just as much part of her life as they were part of theirs.

In August, the weather turned warm. The change was sudden. Within a matter of days, tiny green and white buds shot out of stems. The clouds cleared, and when the sun shone, the air smelled like spring. In the mornings, Kate took the baby for a walk in the pram along the beach. Bilqis walked with her, as it helped overcome the stiffness in her joints. There were few people about at this time except for joggers and people walking their dogs. Sometimes they saw the tiny figure of a swimmer in the distance, plowing through the water. On the misty horizon, tankers moved slowly. Elderly ladies, walking in twos, often stopped by and, peering into the pram, remarked how pretty the baby was.

"Oh look! How much hair she has!" they might say and then, glancing at Bilqis's beaming face, compliment her even more. "What a beautiful grandchild you have! You must be very proud."

The morning walk was a pleasant routine. There was no wind and the bay was placid. Its surface was so still that parts of it reflected the sky. Brown waves lapped at the glistening sand and strands of green and blue seaweed lay washed up as far as the previous tide had come.

The women walked as far as Green Point, occasionally stopping at the Brighton Beach Gardens for a rest. One day, Bilqis and Kate found themselves at the war memorial behind the gardens. Bilqis had seen the stone obelisk from afar but had never stopped by to look at it. *DUCIT AMOR PATRIA* it said under its coat of arms. Behind it, a sandstone wall with the names of the dead: Abbott, Adamson, Addis . . . Banks, Barnes, Barratt . . .

Bilqis looked down the list, wondering if she might find a Muslim or Hindu name among the others. She had read about cameleers who came to Australia nearly a hundred years ago from parts of India and Afghanistan, and wondered if a peripatetic cameeler lay among the fallen soldiers of the First World War. As she looked, she began to notice the double and triple entries under the same name. Allan and Black must have been common names but there were two Blannin-Fergusons, three Blencowes and four Clarks. Were they brothers? What about the five Moores, the three Mcleods and the four entries under Wise? How were they killed? Where were their graves? Were their bodies even in one piece, recognizable, had their mothers set their eyes upon them, their little sons, all grown up now only to be slaughtered far from home? Or were they blown to bits, only preserved whole in memory by those who loved them until they themselves died and there was nothing left?

She sat down on the steps and wrapped her coat tight around her. She had mixed feelings about being here, so far from home. Each time she came here, she had a sense of incredulity, of desecration, as if she were crossing a forbidden border. The highways, skyscrapers and parks reminded her of a reconstituted Europe, but, like the food served on airplanes, there was something ersatz about it, fragile and steely, as if everything were a sham and on the brink of brutality. For the first time, she felt a heartrending sense of pity for this country. It ceased to be foreign and turned into a scarred and battered place, a world forever incomplete, haunted by the dead young men who lay far from its shores. She could feel them all around her. They were very faint, and they had no corporeal substance and were without consciousness, but they were there, like leaves cast about in a wind, or eddies of sand at the bottom of a stream. She felt a momentary shiver of fear, but it passed and then she was left only with a sadness so deep that she let out a gasp.

"What's the matter?" Kate asked, leaning over. "Are you all right?"

"I am okay. I just need a little rest."

Kate pulled up the pram and sat down beside her. She was tired. She had slept badly. She had fed and settled Tara during the night and been awake since dawn, when the baby awoke. There were dark circles beneath her eyes.

"When I was growing up in Calcutta, Sikander used to bring his officer friends from the regiment to stay at our house," Bilqis said. "We used to sit in the garden and have tea with them. I remember the phone ringing, couriers coming and going and orderlies scurrying about with polished boots. It was such a wonderful time. We were young and full of life. No one cared who was what. We were all Indians and that was all that mattered, none of this Hindu and Muslim business. When we migrated to Pakistan, Sikander joined the newly formed army there. They laid out the red carpet for him and gave him a promotion. Within a year, war broke out with India. When he realized that he would be asked to fight his old friends, he resigned. He went to his commanding officer, handed over his pistol and walked away. The commanding officer could have court-martialed him but he knew that Sikander was doing the honorable thing. He saluted him instead and said that it was his great privilege to have known him."

The women were silent. Kate remembered the night when Bilqis and Samad had argued with each other in Urdu. She had felt furious then but she understood now why the conversation had gone that way. Bilqis had traveled halfway around the world to be with her son. It was natural and self-evident that she would feel resentful. It seemed unfair, but wasn't that life, settling some things and unsettling others? In thirty years' time, it could so easily be her turn, she thought. She might be alone, her children far from home, and everything would come back full circle.

"Last night, I dreamed that Tara was dead," Kate said. "I was holding her in my arms and she was exactly like she is now, wrapped in a bundle, but she was dead. Her hair was the hair of a dead child. I woke up and I couldn't go back to sleep. That's what worries me most, the possible death of my child. I see her every day. I feel her breath on my face and I know, I remind myself, that she could be gone tomorrow, wrenched from me the next moment, and I could be looking at the same body except that it would be lifeless and empty. I just hope that I'll die before her. I can imagine my parents dying one day because I can see them growing old and I know that they'll be gone but I can't bear the thought of my child dying."

Bilqis thought about these words for the rest of her stay. They were in her mind when she said good-bye to the family at the airport. She hugged Kate and looked at her. The expression on her face, the look in her eyes, showed no animosity. It occurred to Bilqis then that she understood Kate perfectly. It was true that Kate had conceded nothing, she thought, but she was a mother now and did a mother not ultimately concede everything?

14

BILQIS WAS SITTING up in her bed, knitting a little purple cardigan with tassels from a pattern she had cut out of a magazine. It was the third week of September. She had been back from Melbourne for nearly a fortnight and already the trip seemed like a lifetime ago. Karachi was the same as always. The monsoon had come and gone but not before days and days of rain. At first the rain had come in big drops that turned to hail the size of pebbles. Then came thunder and the downpour that everyone had been expecting. It rolled from one end of the city to the other in sheets, drenching everything, and then vanished over the sea. Steam rose from the hot earth. Soon the gutters were gurgling with storm water, the streets awash with floating sewage. People waded through the water, lifting their trousers above their knees, and big rats, washed out of the drains, did belly flops in the wakes of cars.

Click, click, click. The stitches were getting tighter, she noticed; she was knitting too fast. She breathed deeply and eased her pace. From her bedroom window, she glimpsed the afternoon sky, pale blue and cloudless. It gave her an impression of fair weather, but she could feel the first chill of cold wind blowing from the Baluchi desert that marked the onset of autumn. The

ball of purple yarn fell from her lap and unwound itself on the
floor.

Bilqis put her things away and picked up the book on her bedside table. It was the last of the four-set volume of *Memoirs of the
Life, Exile and Conversations of the Emperor Napoleon* by the Count
de Las Cases. Bilqis had bought the set for Hashmat in Saddar
many years ago. The 1890 American edition was still in impeccable
condition. Its paper was thick. The leather binding protected it so
well that it looked like new. After searching her handbag, Bilqis
fished out her glasses and started to read about Napoleon in exile,
and how he, who had possessed such boundless power and dis-
posed of so many Crowns, occupied a wretched one-room hovel, a
few feet square, perched upon a rock, bereft of furniture and without even shutters or curtains for the windows.

The book resonated with her. It was with a good-hearted zeal that
Samad wished her to move to Australia, but she felt a certain antago-
nism toward him for his disregard for her feelings. She could not
drive. She did not know anyone. Had he considered what life might
be like for her, what she might do, how she might spend her time?
The very thought of living so far away from everything that was familiar and natural to her paralyzed her mind. She had grown up in
the era of the extended family, when parents lived with their children
and their grandchildren in the same house or next to each other.
Times were changing, even in Pakistan, where more and more young
couples were living away from their parents, but until Samad had offered to buy a flat for her, she had not thought that she would have to
leave her home. Sometimes she felt that she had every right to summon him back and demand that he care for her and, at other times,
she thought that she had no rights at all. All she wanted was his love,
but nothing seemed intuitive anymore. Justifications that had been
clear to her became clouded by her ceaseless interpretation of things.

She turned back to her book. Napoleon's humiliation lay not in defeat. It lay in exile, she thought. In a way, leaving was the easy thing to do, but was it not also the humiliating thing to do? If her circumstances were inadequate here, wouldn't she be completely lost elsewhere? Was that not reason enough to stay?

Outside her bedroom window, the trees rustled in a soft breeze. The house was quiet. The door to the balcony was open and the weather was sticky. She could hear fragments of the Friday sermon floating over the air from the faraway mosque, rising and falling with the breeze. "Glory is to him who acknowledges no master but God. Glory is to him whom no earthly delights can sway from prayer . . . to him who forsakes the kingdom of today . . . glory to him who strives to be of service to the Five Holies . . . to him who turns from the world for the song of the desert . . . glory to him who throws away the cup . . . glory, supreme and eternal . . ."

Bilqis was not overtly religious but she had kept the superstitions of someone who from time to time turned to religion. She felt annoyed that she did not hear the last words of the sermon. She wanted so much to rest and awaken to find herself refreshed, all heartache dissolved away. "The peace of the devout," she murmured as she thought of the untroubled happiness of people who rested on God's will. They could begin afresh after each prayer, invigorated by faith that their trials were a sign of God's favor, and that to suffer them in patient submission was a proof of their virtue. "What peace, what bliss!" she thought wistfully, like someone who can no longer feel peace or bliss.

She opened the balcony door and hung her towel on a rack. The grass was growing thick after the monsoon rains. The gardener, as usual, was nowhere to be seen. A pair of noisy crows sat on the overhead electricity line. A dove cooed in the trees. As she was about to return indoors, she caught a blur of red through the leaves. A girl was crossing the road. She was wearing a red kameez and orange shalwar with a black dupatta. Bilqis squinted her eyes and looked closer.

15

IT WAS A short walk across the road to the white villa. Mumtaz rang the bell on the gate and waited for Omar, remembering the first time she had rung it, while Bilqis was in Melbourne. Mumtaz had been talking to Omar on the telephone for many months by then. The phone conversations had become her lifeline. Sometimes the two argued and raised their voices, but the tiffs never lasted long. If they quarreled in the morning they usually made up by noon. Omar was quick to pick fights and quick to make amends, but after one especially heated argument, he stopped calling. Mumtaz had arranged her whole life around his telephone calls. When several weeks went by without any sign of him, she began to wonder if he had gone back to Kashmir.

One day in the bazaar, she saw a small makeshift stall run by a mujahideen group fighting in Kashmir. In the bakery she had seen their red tin donation boxes. But this was something else. They were recruiting volunteers. On a small table lay an open ledger for men to fill in their particulars. Next to the table were two large pieces of cardboard propped up against chairs. One of them showed pictures of dead Indian and Sikh soldiers, and the other equally gruesome pictures of dead mujahideen. Mumtaz became very upset, and found herself imagining the most dreadful things. She had never seen corpses before, not like these, of men who had suffered violent deaths, and their fatal wounds had left them bloodied and torn, like carcasses. It was a horrifying spectacle. She retched over and over again on her way home.

The next day Mumtaz decided to go to the white villa to see if Omar was still there. One foot in front of the other was all it took. A dozen steps from her doorstep to the other would have sufficed, but for the girl the small expanse of road stretched out forever. Its tar glistened in the sun and it seemed as wide as the sea. The air was hot and still. Perspiration appeared on her brow. Fervently she prayed that no one would see her, even when a voice in her head reminded her that, given the circumstances, prayers were actually a little hypocritical. The white villa looked deserted. It was a palatial property built on an immense plot that had been landscaped and planted with grass and palm trees. Rain had washed away the earth here and there, leaving behind craters in the ground. She rang the doorbell. After what seemed like an age, Omar came out. He opened the gate to let her in.

"You're still here," Mumtaz remarked happily. "I thought you had gone."

"Gone where?"

"Gone to fight."

Omar smiled and looked at her. "I didn't go," he said. "I didn't want to, not this time anyway, but it's no good standing here. Come in."

They walked down a lane that ran along the side of the house, Mumtaz following him quietly. Omar opened a side door and nodded at her to enter. Then he looked over his shoulder and bolted the door from inside.

Omar showed her the villa as a curator might take a visitor on a private tour of a museum. It belonged to a businessman who had risen from obscurity to fortune in a matter of a few years as a result of the poppy trade from Afghanistan. In expatiation, he gave alms to charities. The good work rendered him immune to slander. He and his family now lived somewhere in Virginia, where they owned a four-acre property with its own duck pond. They visited Karachi every few years. Between visits the villa remained closed. In the stuffy, airless spaces, the sofas had gone musty, the mattresses hard.

Omar and Mumtaz wandered from room to room. It was all a game and would have been quite harmless were it not for the undercurrent of desire that restraint made even stronger. Each room they crossed brought them a little nearer to danger. Finally, they came to Omar's room. It was at the back of the house, with cobwebs in the corners of the ceiling and a blind window that faced the perimeter wall. There was little furniture here, just a charpoy and a television set. The blades of the ceiling fan were black with grime. A side table held an ashtray, a pack of cigarettes and a newspaper. On the mantelpiece lay a plastic comb, books and some letters.

"So this is where you live," Mumtaz remarked.

"This is it."

"You didn't finish telling me why you didn't go."

"It didn't seem right."

"Why not?"

"Because of you. It's your fault."

"Why—what have I done wrong?"

"Everything! You filled me with doubts. I never used to be so indecisive. You managed to confuse me completely."

"You spoke to me first, remember? You didn't have to."

"You're right. It's my fault then."

"Should I go away?"

Omar beckoned her to sit down on the bed. When she remained standing, he leaned over to touch her brow. Mumtaz stared at him but said nothing. His hand dared linger a little longer at the wave of hair that had escaped from her shawl. His courage began to rise. He sat down on his bed and asked her to sit beside him. Mumtaz glanced around. They were completely alone. No one knew that she was here. She did not have to hurry home. After gravely considering his request, she smiled. She drew her breath and sat down.

How brave she is, Omar thought. He touched her hand and stroked the inside of her arm. Then he put his arm around her and, gently turning her face toward him, kissed her on the mouth. Mumtaz sat very still, looking at him as he kissed her. It felt silly. She could sense his awkwardness too. He seemed so vulnerable that she felt she could push him away with her finger, but she did not stop him. She wanted him. She needed to see him whole. More kisses followed. She let him hug her. As he started to take off her kameez, she panicked and began to sob. For at least half an hour, she sat there in her blouse, as tears poured down her face. She told him what a bad person she was and how much she hated herself.

Omar bowed his head and listened. He wanted to reassure her. She was a good girl, a circumspect girl. She had not come here instantly, in one jump. His machinations had brought her here. He did not dare frighten her now. His heart beat rapidly. He did not say much and waited. When she had quieted down, he hugged and kissed her again. These kisses had a different flavor. They were long, lingering and passionate. He undid the drawstring on her shalwar and let it fall. He lay her down, and took her blouse over her arms. With both hands, he spread her legs. Then he undid his shalwar and pushed himself into her. She locked eyes with him. Tears flowed down her face once more but she reached up and drew him closer. She raised her head and watched with awe and fascination as he thrust into her, moving convulsively between her thighs. Her hands went to his hips and rested there.

It became easier after the first time. Mumtaz lost her inhibitions.

Within weeks, she went from being remorseful and guilt-ridden about sex to wanting it. Sex was no longer abominable. It fed her. It completed her. They were so unlike anyone else, the two of them, loved by nobody and not seeking anyone's sympathy. They had the right to be with each other. Every time she went to be with him, she could forget herself. The hoarse cries of her mother, the orders of her mistress, all those nuisances that blotted her existence fell away. There were nights when she could not sleep; her thin mattress seemed like concrete, so restless did she feel with desire. She had never known her body to possess such strong needs.

She met Omar every week or so, always in the afternoon. It was no longer a moral struggle for her—the taboo had been breached. It became something else now, outside morality and outside faith. The two grew bolder and became more playful with each other. Some days they made love so often that their bodies ached afterward. Often they went into a walled garden that belonged to the white villa, with bougainvillea creepers in different shades along the walls and a grove of fiery red gulmohar trees. Here their isolation was complete. They would pull out their charpoy under the shade of the trees and drowsily lie together, talking in quiet tones. The secrecy of their affair heightened their senses and blessed their interaction with an intensity and excitement that would have been impossible otherwise. The quietness of the place and the complete solitude wove its own spell. Hours could pass by without their realizing, until the muezzin's call for prayers brought them back to reality. They would pull back in atonement then, but there was always a sense of complicity to their withdrawal, as if they were pleased with their defiance.

Omar, being the more devout of the two, felt the pang of guilt more keenly. How could he sin and pray at the same time? To think that he was a Muslim! How far he had fallen! Every time he had sex with Mumtaz, he washed and scrubbed himself to feel clean again. Full of remorse, he would go to the mosque and stay after the others had left, kneeling in prayer, his forehead pressed to the floor, begging God for forgiveness for what he had done. God knew what was in the hearts of men. Men were human beings and human beings erred.

Every time, he forbade himself from seeing her again, but in a few days his resolve weakened. He told himself that God would understand, and he found himself in her arms again. The joy of entering her and becoming one with her was incomparable to anything he had ever known. The more intimate and familiar he became with her, the greater was the intensity of his pleasure. Sometimes he wished he knew someone who could tell him that he was not as dissolute as he thought he was. But he was too ashamed to tell anyone. And who would he confide in anyway? He had no confidants, no friends. Those he knew at the mosque thought he was one of God's true soldiers. And he liked that image. It made him feel worthy. He did not want anyone to know how weak, how lonely he really was. That's what Mumtaz was for. She drove away his loneliness. She gave him company, but she gave him her body too, and did that not put him in her power?

These thoughts went round and round in his mind. He knew that it was all madness. He should never have spoken to her and ought to stop seeing her at once. But he did nothing of the sort, because he knew that God's judgment would come, and he would pay the price. After all, he had never been so ripe for redemption.

16

MUMTAZ WAS DUSTING the furniture. The morning light streamed into the drawing room through the windows. When she finished, she mopped the floors, washed the dirty rag under the tap and hung it on the line outside to dry.

Bilqis watched her intently from the dining table. It was an exercise in futility, she thought. The dust would rearrange itself and the room would be no cleaner.

"Make sure you clean the picture frames," she said. "There is dust on the photographs."

Mumtaz went about her work with a stony face. She knew that Bilqis was not fastidious about such minor things. If she was chastising her, it was a sign that something else was wrong. Perhaps she suspected something. Was she going to interrogate her too? A random series of questions and answers flashed through her mind. When Bilqis summoned her after finishing breakfast, she was ready.

"Tell me, Mumtaz," Bilqis remarked, examining a faint crack in her porcelain cup. "Tell me, that man across the road . . . do you know him?"

"Which man, begum sahiba?" the girl exclaimed.

"The man who is always coming around to do errands. You know which one."

"The chowkidar?"

"Are you having an affair?"

The girl swore that such a thing was untrue.

"Suppose you tell me the truth. Who do you speak to on the telephone?"

"Nobody."

"I pick up the phone and the line goes dead. Why?"

"How am I supposed to know?" Mumtaz remarked sharply. "It's probably some crank caller."

Bilqis produced a printout and held it up for the girl to see. "I have here a list of numbers from the exchange. I know who has been calling my number. I know the length of each phone call, the day, the hour, down to the last minute. The phone positively hums while I am away. Do you think I am oblivious to what goes on in my house?"

"I have done nothing wrong," the girl said. She gave her mistress a darting glance, as if she were insulted for being called to account. There was something so outlandish about her denial that for a moment Bilqis found herself doubting her own senses, even though she had seen her meet the chowkidar with her own eyes. She wasn't dreaming. She couldn't have imagined it, but what proof did she have? If the girl did not confess, she would have to summon the chowkidar and try to extract the confession out of him. If they both denied her charges, then there was nothing left in her arsenal except threats. She could report the girl to her parents; she could report both of them to the police. No one would doubt her word against theirs.

The only problem was that she could not report them without bringing down the worst possible consequences upon them. The poor girl would be crushed. If she was lucky, she would be packed away at once and married off, but her father would disown her and her brothers would never speak to her again. As for the chowkidar, the police would beat him—that is, if the girl's brothers did not avenge her honor by murdering him. But even if he lived, even if he was sent to jail, he could languish there forever, since no one cared for people like him. Jail would be living death for him.

"Did you meet him yesterday?" Bilqis asked. "I saw you cross the road. He opened the gate for you. Don't lie to me."

Mumtaz blushed deeply and let out a sob. Slowly, details of the entanglement emerged. Bilqis had to extract them little by little, one incident, one anecdote at a time, but they came. She listened to the indiscretions with mute restraint. The girl's nonchalance was gone now. She had turned into a frightened creature who was trying to recognize herself in her own narrative, almost in disbelief, as if she could not reconcile the two.

Bilqis closed her eyes in an expression of grim reproach. "You will forget him," she said, with as dispassionate a voice as she could muster.

Mumtaz hid her face and sobbed for a while. Then a transformation occurred. She wiped her tears and her expression hardened. She would do penance for the rest of her life, she said, but she would do so happily.

"I shall never forget him," she added. "It's the only time in my life that I've felt what it is like to be alive, and I know that I'll never be so happy again."

"What if I tell your mother?"

"Tell her," she blurted out. "She can do with me what she pleases but she can't change the past. She can't change my feelings. What's done is done and I have no regrets."

"This is really going too far," Bilqis said. "First you lie to me and then you challenge me. You show no remorse even though you've done wrong. You say that you'll do penance, but you tell me that you are unrepentant. Who do you think you are?"

Mumtaz stood with her head bowed. When Bilqis made a gesture, she picked up the tea things and went into the kitchen. Her movements were slow and dull, her spark gone. Bilqis watched her leave. In spite of appearing cross, she could not bring herself to be angry with her. Foolish girl, she thought. How could she be so heedless? If word got out, her future would be bleak.

Her fate was now in Bilqis's hands. She could arrange a speedy marriage with her cousin before the whole thing unraveled itself, or she could see if this lover of hers would marry her. In any event, she had to do the right thing by Mumtaz. If she sanctioned marriage, then she had to know that it was a pure and good thing for her. Otherwise it would be nothing but tyranny, and the destruction of all that is holy that must exist between man and wife. How could she sanctify such an arrangement, except on the altar of tradition? Tradition indeed! And what did that make her? An accomplice to tyranny? A despot; a benevolent and just despot, but a despot all the same.

In the evening, Bilqis sent for Omar. Hameeda's grandson was playing marbles in the garden and she used him as her messenger. Omar arrived wearing leather sandals and a white shalwar kameez. A good-looking fellow, Bilqis thought. She could see how Mumtaz had fallen for him.

"You know why I have called you here," she said sternly. "Mumtaz has told me everything. I am sure that you have your own version of the story, but you can spare me that for now. I thought that you were a decent young man. I thought that I could trust you. I made a mistake. I had no idea that you were a bad person. Had I known that you had your eyes on my girl, I would have sorted you out long ago."

"You don't know me, begum sahiba," Omar replied. "You accuse me without giving me a chance to defend myself. I'm not like that."

"Don't you dare look at me in that way," Bilqis said angrily. "I know what I need to know. The law can be very severe."

"The law is not divine," Omar said. "It is made by men, and men are unjust. As God is my witness and my judge, I am answerable only to Him."

Bilqis lost her temper. Her eyes blurred with tears. "The injustice of what you have done has happened in this world and it will be dealt with in this world," she said. "Mumtaz is a good girl. She comes from good people. When you were having your fun with her, did you ever stop to think of the consequences? Did you anticipate the hurt, the pain and the suffering that your actions would bring? Perhaps you thought that you could soil a woman's reputation and evade all responsibility because you are a stranger here. You can vanish overnight and no one will ever be able to find you again. Was that your plan?"

Omar said nothing. His thin face looked severe and implacable, as he stood there shifting from one foot to the other. Bilqis looked at his hands and his fresh, rosy complexion. He seemed lost to her, and she thought of his mother and how far he was from home. She wondered if he was in love with the girl.

"Have you thought of marrying her?" she asked.

"They'd never marry their daughter to a Kashmiri," he said. "They are Pathans. We are beneath them."

"What if I make arrangements?"

"What arrangements?" Omar lifted his eyebrows. He had anxious eyes.

"What if I tell the girl's mother that she is to give her hand in marriage only to someone she agrees to?"

"You do what you like, begum sahiba," he said, shrugging. "It's not what you or I do that's going to matter. In the end, it's only God's will that will be done."

Bilqis drew breath. "I am not entirely sure what your feelings are for Mumtaz," she said. "Perhaps you should go away for a while and let things blow over. Think about your intentions and how you feel about her. She is not a plaything. You can't tamper with her life and move on when you get bored. Think long and hard about what you want to do. What is your will? God's will is done once man has done his part."

Omar was dismissed with the flick of a hand. He walked to the aquarium by the seaside and, for several hours, he strolled around aimlessly, looking at the fish tanks in the curved white walls. In the center of the building there was a small round pond with a stingray inside it. Omar watched the fish for a long time as it swam around in circles, and felt cruel for having bought an admission ticket. Animals were kept in captivity for people like him, he thought. They should be free. They should run wild. As he walked back to the white villa, the scorn he felt for himself equaled the scorn he felt for Mumtaz. She gave him pleasure and made him feel happy but she also made demands on him. Her body, her warmth, her sensuality and her companionship, all those things that brought her close to him, were the same things that repelled him. Women complicated matters, he thought. They imprisoned men and made them weak. The path without shame was without women.

The next day, it was Hameeda's turn. Hameeda was arranging roses in a vase and putting them on the side table in Bilqis's bedroom. Bilqis liked roses but the scent was overpowering. She crooked her finger and asked the woman to come near.

"Where is Mumtaz?" she asked.

"Where I left her, begum sahiba, in the servant quarter, I expect."

Bilqis gave her a pained look. "You must show her your love," she said. "Children grow up and then it is too late. They will reproach you later for it. They will be indignant, but you won't be able to tell them because words will never make up for what you did not show them. There will be no remedy for it because you can't rectify what you did not do."

When she noticed Hameeda looking at her blankly, she felt embarrassed. There was no use being sentimental with her, she thought. It all fell on stony ground. In a brusque voice, she demanded a glass of water. When the woman returned, Bilqis motioned for her to sit down.

"You must promise me, Hameeda, that what I am about to tell you stays within these four walls," she said. "You are not to speak a word of this conversation to anyone, not to your husband, not to your sons and least of all to Mumtaz. Promise me that. Promise me that you will not pass on anything to her. What I tell you is only between you and me. The girl must not know that you know. You will not reprimand her, ever. Promise me that."

She sipped her water and then, her head still full of doubts, she began to reveal her conversation with Mumtaz. Hameeda did not say a word at first. Then she sighed and exploded. "The girl is a whore! My own daughter, a slut! She has ruined my family and rubbed our name in dung. Our faces are blackened. I knew something like this would happen. I knew it. I could see it in her gimlet eyes. She had wickedness written all over her face. I should have washed my hands of her a long time ago. Oh God! What are we going to do?"

Bilqis waited for the fusillade to pass. "Now, Hameeda, don't be a fool," she said. "The girl is not a slut. She may be in love with the man. That does not make her a slut. If she is a slut then she blackens my good name too. She has erred, but she has not sinned. It is the men who ought to suffer. It is they who bring women to sin."

"Fine then," Hameeda sobbed, beating her chest. "Give this man to me. I will bring him to justice."

"We don't want that kind of justice. And you—you will not raise your voice with me . . ." Bilqis raised her own voice. "Do I make myself clear?"

Hameeda wiped her nose with the hem of her kameez. "We have lost everything today, begum sahiba. We are poor. Now we don't even have our honor anymore and you are telling us that we can't avenge ourselves?"

Bilqis ran a finger along the edge of her bed. Its green cover reminded her of a blue-green bottle of Valium. "It pains me, Hameeda, but two wrongs don't make a right," she said. "A long time ago, I promised you that I would take care of the girl's dowry. I am sure you remember. You should also remember that I placed no condition upon you. That is not to say that it was an unconditional promise. No, please don't argue. You know me very well. That was not my intention. I placed no condition because I wanted to keep that right for a later time. That time, I am afraid, is upon us now. I want you to know that you will not coerce her into marriage. You will heed her wishes. You will not go against them. No matter if I am there to remind you, you will respect her decision. That is my condition. I must also say that I don't like to speak like this, for it gives me no pleasure, but I would rather that there be no misunderstanding between us. Let her make her own destiny. If she wants to marry the chowkidar, then let that be. Let her not hold us accountable for making her do something she does not want. It is too heavy a burden to bear. The things that you set in motion have unintended consequences. They always do. All that is left behind is the resentment and anger of those whom you tried to steer, even if you did so out of good will."

Bilqis fetched her handbag and took out five crisp hundred-rupee notes. She pressed them into the woman's hand. "Girls are a heavy burden, Hameeda," she continued. "That's why I don't want your menfolk to know. Sometimes the less they know, the better it is. They will not benefit from this knowledge, except for using it as justification for their own grievances, real and imagined. That's why I must ask you to uphold a vow of silence."

Hameeda sat on her haunches, making a low howling noise like a wounded cat, but she was reassured by her employer's manner. It was like the blazing sun that had shown itself from behind the clouds. She was sniffling when she went out into the sun herself, and began weeping once more when she reached her own door, but a few hours later, when she squatted down to milk her goat, her dark mood began to lift. She pulled the plump, taut teats with long, vengeful strokes. A good beating is what that silly daughter of hers needed now. Her palms ached to give her a few well-deserved slaps, but she would do nothing and say nothing, she thought. The truth was that she did not care whom Mumtaz married. As long as there was no scandal, the matter was irrelevant. If she married the chowkidar, so much the better for her. It was better to be married to a younger man than an older one, she thought. God knew that she knew—when was the last time that her husband's hand had held her breasts? The good news was that the dowry was taken care of. Things were not so squalid after all. "I will take care of it"—the words, like a mantra, restored her faith in her employer. Bilqis had let her son drift and marry that white floozy—that's what the people called her—but today she had vindicated herself in Hameeda's eyes. She was her old self again, and that made Hameeda proud of her.

17

THE NEXT MORNING, Mumtaz was moping in the kitchen when Omar appeared at the door. It was ten o'clock. The house was empty. Mumtaz let him in and allowed him to sit down on a stool. It was a difficult moment because she had a premonition of why he was here. Although she was pale and a little drawn, she also felt strong and resolute. A day had gone by without incident. Hameeda had not said anything to her. In fact, she had been uncharacteristically quiet and restrained. She had not even looked Mumtaz in the eye, which meant that she knew about the affair but Bilqis had sealed her lips. Mumtaz felt safe, unafraid of the world changing around her and the turmoil that it would bring into her life. She boiled a kettle of water and made him a cup of tea.

The sky was overcast. Streaks of sunshine pierced through the luminous clouds. A few drops of rain pattered on the ground and the sun came out. "The foxes are getting married," Omar joked. They laughed together. Mumtaz was surprised at how mildly he spoke. He said very little otherwise. There was none of his old bravado.

"I'll be going home soon," he told her. "I'll stay there for winter this time and when the weather turns warm, I'll go to fight."

"I know."

"I am not sure when I'll be back again."

"You do what you must."

"Do I have your permission?"

"My permission? You've never asked for it before. Why ask for it now?"

"If you tell me not to go, I won't go."

"You won't be happy here," she said. She did not wish to compromise him, but her voice was weary. "You should follow your heart."

Omar lifted up his head and gave a long sigh. His suffering seemed at its height. "I wrote something for you," he finally said, a little more sprightly, and rolled out a piece of paper. He glanced at her once more and then turned to his writing.

> *Upon my shroud with my heart's blood, I write:*
> *The nightingales will sing of our love, I promise*
> *The fervour of my love will be honey on your lips, I promise*
> *Don't forget me, my beloved, don't forget me*
> *Lest I fly into a candle's flame;*
> *For at least she, with tears of grief, will remember me.*

"My warrior poet," Mumtaz said. She said it simply, without clamoring or imploring him.

Omar looked at her, as if saying, "In this life, we must do what we must; but in the next life, we will do what we please."

Her eyes were cast down. He gave her a nod and, without saying another word, left the way he had come. There was no kiss, no parting embrace. None was expected. A declaration of love would have been superfluous, even crude. She went back to her work. She was glad to be alone. The empty house seemed warm and cozy, its silence wonderful, but no sooner did her mind start to grow peaceful again than she realized she had lost him. There was a great difference between not seeing someone indefinitely and never seeing someone again. The thoughts that had consoled her a moment ago now vanished into the ether. The tips of her fingers started to feel cold. She thought she might collapse, and she had to summon all her will to keep from falling. Then her strength gave out, and she sat down against the wall and wept.

Winter came. Mumtaz waited but there was no word from Omar, no telephone calls, not even a letter or telegram to say how he was. As time passed, her feelings for him began to fade. Love tipped over into anger and resentment. She felt that he had come into her life by accident and changed it forever, that he had not understood her much, nor cared to. He had a fanatical view of things, and he did in the end what he had always wanted to do. Why did she have to live her life defined by him? Why did she have to see herself as the victim, as the abandoned one, the betrayed one, when that would have been his ultimate triumph, to make her a martyr too? Why did she have to carry his legacy when she owed him nothing? The strange thing was that she could not feel angry with him without feeling angry with herself. She could not hate him without hating herself. The rapture and memory of her love still lived inside her.

In February, nearly four months after Omar went away, Mumtaz received a letter, in which he wrote about how happy his mother was to have him back home. She never wanted him to leave again. She wanted him to marry some Kashmiri girl and settle down close by, but the fact was that his mother did not understand the secret currents of his life. She understood nothing. Some men married and others didn't. A man's goal in life was to find his destiny, not to marry and have children. His conscience could not permit him to marry anyone except Mumtaz and he could not marry her because of his cause. He wrote that he loved her but his heart was not in marriage. If he married her, he would fail her, and he could not fail her. With these words, he urged her to forget him.

18

THE FIGHTERS CROSSED over into Indian territory at dawn. A dozen artillery pieces from the Pakistani side gave them covering fire. The roar of guns was deafening. The air was filled with the whine of shells flying above them to pound the Indian positions ahead. The Indian patrols kept a close eye on the goat paths that zigzagged down the mountainside, but thanks to the artillery fire they were pinned down in their deep, well-camouflaged bunkers. The fighters encountered no resistance. They found their path quickly, as they recognized landmarks from the previous year. They were used to these crossings. Some of them went over the Line of Control several times a year. In forty-five minutes, they navigated their way past the Indian lookouts. As if on cue, the guns fell silent.

It was early spring. The ground was hard, emerging from the winter thaw. There were traces of muddy snow in the shadows. The fighters talked in low, soft voices and puffed into their hands to keep them warm. They wore dark woolen shawls that they had wrapped over their thin shalwar kameez. A few were clad in cheap green anoraks, their faces partly covered. Several of them wore sandals, others an assortment of tattered running shoes and army boots. Their Kalashnikovs were slung over their shoulders.

They started climbing a ridge covered with edelweiss. It was a long ascent but since they were young and carried little weight, they scrambled uphill without effort. Behind them, they could see clouds of black smoke rising where the shells had fallen. When they reached the top of the ridge, they found themselves standing at the edge of a forest. The air was filled with birdsong. All around them was an immense vista of mountains. The valley lay cradled below, startlingly beautiful. It was a perfect morning. In the majestic calm of their surrounds, it was difficult to apprehend the savage bombardment of a few hours ago.

The men were elated, as if on the verge of coming home. They enjoyed a sense of camaraderie and felt comfortable around their leader. Abu Ammar was a legend among them, who year after year had led his men in and out of danger without a scratch. It was as if God were watching over him. There were ten of them in all. Five were insurgents from Indian Kashmir with personal scores to settle: a missing brother whom the Indians took away and never released; a sister raped in an army camp; a parent shot dead without cause. They were used to coming and going to the Pakistani side for firearms and training.

The Pakistani men were a mixed bunch. From Lahore, there was a doctor in his early twenties. He belonged to a religious party and was here for ideological reasons but he had an easygoing manner and was the comedian of the group. From Faisalabad, there were two tradesmen, a plumber and a mechanic. The plumber was a swarthy man with a pockmarked face, in his late twenties, unmarried, and the sole provider for his mother and two siblings. The mechanic was a gaunt, tall and earnest fellow with glittering black eyes. Both were veterans from previous campaigns. Unlike the doctor, they were not motivated by religion. They had come to fight because they believed in the Kashmiri cause. It gave meaning to their lives.

The fourth fighter was a young journalist from Karachi who had come with romantic notions of adventure. In his rucksack he had brought along pencils, notepads and a camera. He had told his parents that he was going hiking with friends in the Himalayas. The others chided him and called him a dandy, because he was the youngest and most delicate among them. And then, of course, there was their leader, Omar, whose nom de guerre was Abu Ammar.

Around noon, they stopped by a stream for a simple meal from their supplies. A few of them took off their shoes and prayed with their weapons beside them while others smoked cigarettes and talked in quiet tones, laughing occasionally. Their trek resumed after lunch and continued for several hours. Toward evening they arrived at a remote village, where they stopped at a small house. The village was perched on the side of a deep ravine. From time to time, a high wind swept down the gorge and covered everything with a film of dust.

The fighters settled themselves in a room with a bare earthen floor. Its cold, hard clay surface had been swept clean. A couple of tall brooms stood in a corner. They waited for the owner of the house, Omar's uncle. It was dark outside when he appeared with a lantern. He left it hanging from a hook in the door as he turned to face his visitors. Omar stood up and bowed slightly. The old man was tall and bald, with a small beard that he had dyed with henna. It made his dark, leathery face appear even darker.

Omar put his hand on his heart. The others were tired from their journey, but following their leader's example, they also rose to their feet to greet their host. The old man nodded and made a sign for them to be seated, then reached out and patted his nephew on his head.

"How are things?" Omar asked after everyone had sat down.

The old man smiled. It pleased him to see his nephew. He was endangering his family by taking in the fighters, but he considered it his duty. The boy was brave, like the old man used to be.

"Did you meet any sentries along the way?"

"Not this time," Omar said, "but they've never given us any trouble. We bribe them to let us pass. Why?"

"Things are not good," said the old man. "The Indians know when the fighters come and go."

"Do you have spies in the village?"

"It's a Muslim village. Everyone knows one another."

"It only takes one."

The old man frowned. He knew it to be true.

"Two weeks ago, a busload of Indian soldiers came," he said. "They searched every house for weapons. When they found nothing, they shot the cattle and set fire to the hay. A girl from the village was taken away in a truck. We found her the next morning. She was alive but her face was covered with scratches. No one is safe."

"We won't come again," Omar said. "We'll take another route."

"And put yourselves in harm's way?"

"Better us than you."

"While I live, you will come to my house," said the old man. "You bring me happiness. I too have killed men in my time and sent them to hell, and would not hesitate to go with you if I was young again. The least I can do is to condone what you are doing and bless you to God."

Omar's aunt, an elderly woman, brought out a tray with tin plates, loaves of bread and a bowl of curry. Omar dipped a little of the bread in curry and ate. He had lost his appetite. The food had a little grit in it, but he didn't mind the grit. It was the account of atrocities that had filled him with revulsion. The other men went on eating. Omar's young cousin came in to collect the plates. She kept her gaze low and did not look at the visitors. While she moved about, the fighters were also careful not to raise their eyes, but Omar exchanged a quick, playful glance with her. He was fond of the girl and felt a little sad seeing how fast she was growing up.

Even a year ago she had been a child. Was it really fifteen years ago that her mother used to carry her down to the river where their families used to meet? Soon she would go into purdah. Then she would be married and he would never see her again. What if the Indians took her, just like they had taken that other girl? He closed his eyes in horror.

Omar's aunt returned with quilts and blankets. His uncle threw more wood into the fireplace. When the fire was roaring, he bade his guests good night and retired. As the men lay down to rest, Omar remained awake. Anger swept over him and then a sense of loss, the feeling that time had betrayed him and cut him and taken away the things that were dearest to him. No matter what one did, the world ultimately broke one's heart. Life was folly, he thought, illuminated by nothing except feeble hopes. Desire was folly. Hope was folly. Was not everything folly? Even his own body, fleshy and lustful? What else did he have in the face of oblivion, except folly?

The men slept fully dressed. Toward daybreak, Omar was the first to awake. His aunt brought him a basin of warm water. He went outside and sat down by the edge of a narrow drain that ran alongside the house. He washed his face, hands and feet. After drying himself with a towel, he returned indoors to offer his prayers. In the morning stillness, he could hear his uncle reciting the Koran. Omar had read the Koran as a youngster. Although he did not understand Arabic, he recognized the verse because he knew it by rote. It was Soora-e-Asra: *"We have made the destiny of every human being cling to his neck and we shall bring forth for him on the Day of Resurrection a book which he will find wide open . . ."*

He listened to his uncle reciting the sacred words in his sonorous voice. When he finished, the house fell quiet again. A rooster started crowing in the yard. Omar felt wonderfully light. The morning sounds filled him with happiness. Despite having slept poorly, he was not tired. He examined his gun, ammunition packs and grenades. The fighters were planning to dynamite a communications tower located in a glade not ten miles from the village. Omar questioned his uncle about the road and the number of enemy he was likely to encounter there. He embraced the old man as he and his fighters set out to leave. As the sun rose, the sky turned blue, cloudless as far as the eye could see.

The Indian post was in a clearing at the edge of the forest. When the fighters reached their goal, Omar found a hiding place in the tree line and peered through his binoculars. The post was defended by a dozen or so soldiers. One of them stood behind a machine-gun emplacement but the others milled around, listening to a radio, shaving, writing letters. Omar split eight of the fighters into two parties of four. They were to ambush the emplacement from the flanks while he and another fighter gave them covering fire from the tree line. As the fighters started to slip away, the Indians spotted the movement. A burst of heavy machine-gun fire followed one of the men, who was trailing behind the others. The bullets kicked up dirt under his feet but he rolled and escaped.

"Fuckers!" he grunted.

The other men laughed. Bullets did not frighten them.

Omar fired several rounds, and then emptied his chamber with a full burst. He pulled out another clip from his pouch and jammed it into his gun. He was sitting down, balancing on a knee and taking aim with one eye closed, as he used to when killing birds with his slingshot. He could not miss. As he fired again and again, Mumtaz's face appeared in front of his eyes. Her hot breath fell on his neck and he was reminded of the targets he had shot at the circus with her. Bullets flew past him without touching him. He felt no remorse in killing. It was as if his body had ceased to exist. Only the consciousness of taking aim and firing remained. And elation.

The gun battle ended in victory for the fighters. They overran the enemy post and started laying charges around the communication tower to blow it up. They had to step over corpses as they dragged a spool of wire around for the detonator. Some of the enemy soldiers were still alive but wounded, moaning and asking for water. Progress was slow. Suddenly they heard a faraway screech that came closer and closer. A mortar bomb exploded several hundred yards to their left. More mortar bombs whistled through the air, exploding fifty yards away, then another burst only ten or twenty yards away. The whine got closer and closer, increasing in pitch. "Get down!" Omar screamed as he realized that the Indians were bracketing them left and right. They had been ambushed. As soon as there was a lull, the men got up and retreated.

They ran fast. The ground was damp and springy beneath their feet. Snow glinted on faraway peaks. The air was bracing. Eagles wheeled above them. Suddenly there was a muffled explosion, a loud crump sound, and the journalist was thrown many feet into the air. He fell down hard on the ground and lay very still. Then he sat up slowly and looked around with a puzzled expression, his face covered with dust and blood. His leg was missing below the knee. Blood gushed from the wound. He slapped his knee in disbelief, saying, "Where is my leg, where is my leg?" Then his face went white and the pupils began to dilate. *Thump, thump, thump,* went the mortar rounds all around them, as shrapnel and pieces of sod flew through the air. The plumber was hit next. He lay holding a hand to his neck. His breathing became labored and then he exhaled and was dead. Omar moved his hand and saw a small neat hole the size of a coin on one side of his neck. The other side of his neck was gone. One of the Kashmiri fighters had been shot through the abdomen. He lay doubled up, whimpering, his tunic drenched in blood. He was a young, handsome boy with blue-green eyes that were now screwed up in agony. Omar gave him a drink from his bottle. There was nothing more he could do.

He could hear the Indians up on a hillside jabbering. They were talking in Punjabi, saying how they were going to kill him. Every particle of his body screamed at him to flee, but he forced himself to stay. His hands shook as he and the doctor bandaged the journalist as best they could. The doctor bantered with him and for a while it seemed that the journalist was laughing, but he was actually grimacing with pain. The doctor gave him a morphine shot.

"Don't worry," Omar said to him. "We're going home now. Home, do you understand? Everything is going to be all right."

Hollow words, shallow and meaningless. It was hard to believe that his men had been alive only a few minutes ago—each one breathing, living, thinking. When they had awoken that morning, did they contemplate that death was going to come not in old age, not in forty or fifty years, but in a few hours? Had they trusted their fate? Had each of them believed that death could not strike him down? That he would be spared, that death wouldn't get the better of him?

Omar staggered away from the scene of slaughter and vomited in a nearby ditch. It was a good thing, he thought, that Mumtaz was not seeing him in this state. He had been happy with her. Their time together was brief but now it seemed endless, like those summers from his childhood and adolescence that felt as if they had lasted forever. It was a fitting punishment, he thought, to see things in their true light when it was too late.

After a minute or two he went back and told his men that they weren't going to leave the journalist behind. There was no question of his falling into Indian hands. He lifted him up like a sack and carried him on his back. One by one, the remaining men overtook him and went into the dense foliage ahead, where they were safe. The mechanic and Omar took turns carrying the wounded man. They went along a gentle trough that rolled down into a small meadow hemmed in by trees, following an ever-steepening trail that wound down the mountainside. A green snake rustled through the grass a few feet ahead of them. The air smelled fresh and sounds carried far. Omar could hear the Indians in pursuit. They seemed far away, but then he heard their voices close by, the sergeants shouting orders, jamming magazines into their rifles and firing. Bullets whipped past him and slammed into trees.

The Indians, unfamiliar with the terrain, began to fall behind. Omar's trio caught up with the rest of his group and trudged along, dwarfed by tall chinar trees. Every now and then he paused to look for the trail, which was uneven, at times steep and at times flat. The shadows lengthened, then dusk fell and the air turned cold. The fighters were accustomed to moving by night. After they had walked for some time, Omar dropped away from the others and listened. Except for the harsh breathing of the dying journalist, he could hear nothing. He joined the others and ordered them to wait under a clump of trees. His leg muscles twitched with exhaustion. His shirt clung to his back, soaked with blood. He lay the journalist down on the grass and covered him with a thin blanket. The night glittered with stars. The Milky Way was glowing like a long, luminous cloud. A meteor appeared. The moon rose. The rocks and the muddy snow shone in its pale light. The journalist was shivering and grinding his teeth. The other men gave him a piece of rope to bite on. Pungent sweat drenched his clothes. He became manic and started to scream, hurling obscenities at everyone. Omar told the others to leave him alone. They were silent as the journalist swore long and hard at God. Then he lost consciousness, and his body started to turn cold.

He was a nice young man, undoubtedly from a wealthy family, and was intelligent and kind, the sort who is fundamentally incapable of violence. Now he was dead when he least deserved it.

When he began his soliloquy of abuse, addressing God with the singular "tu," Omar felt a wicked sense of satisfaction. It was as if, hearing the other man's words, his own half-hearted rebellion was assuaged. Where was His clement, merciful God now, when His faithful needed Him most? If He was so omniscient, so powerful, then why was He incapable of interfering in human affairs? Why did He permit so much suffering? Or was He a weak God, incapable of altering the universe He had created? Trials, yes, God puts His faithful through trials—that's what the faithful would have told him, but was it not possible, however improbable, that He had no choice but to let things be the way they had to be? If He had no choice, if the world could be no different, then why was He necessary? Why was He to be worshipped?

Toward midnight, the men heard shells falling a long way off. Then, like a dim thunder rolling forward, the barrage swept toward them. Great chunks of tree bark flew through the air. The entire forest seemed on fire and the earth was chewed up by shell bursts. As they ran for cover, it seemed they were wading through a freshly plowed pit. The darkness was lit up every now and then by the flash of explosions. There were sheets of flame rising all around them. Their ears were deafened, their eyes stung and their minds were paralyzed by fear. In the flashes of light and, after each shell burst, they could see silhouettes of Indian soldiers.

The guns fired all night. With dawn, the long-range Bofors guns on the Pakistani side opened up. Each time a round slammed through the canopy of trees, the explosion sent shock waves through the air. As the sky grew light, everything became serene again. A great silence descended. Wood smoke drifted up the valley. The air carried with it the faraway sound of bleating goats. The forest was awash with the scent of damp soil, slightly pungent from the pine needles mingling with leaves and clay and blood into the substance of the mountain itself.

Omar lay still on the frost-covered grass. His body was thrown on its side, his head turned, as if in sleep. His cold fist clutched the Kalashnikov that lay beside him. As the sun rose across the distant Pir Panjal ranges, it shone through the treetops, and turned the frost into dew.

19

TIME PASSED. BILQIS waited for a letter from Omar or his elders, but when spring came to an end and there was still no news, she was convinced that her doubts were well founded. Omar was a bad character. He never had any intention of marrying Mumtaz. She had been a fool to think that he might have been in love with her. To put her mind at rest, however, she decided to have a quiet word with Mumtaz and ask if she had heard from him. To her surprise, Mumtaz burst into tears at the mention of his name.

"He was a mujahid, begum sahiba, fighting in Kashmir," she said.

"I did not know."

"He did not tell everyone. He used to go during summer. That's why we only saw him here in winter. He was away fighting the rest of the time."

"Did you always know?"

Mumtaz nodded. "I used to warn him that he would get killed but I could not stop him. Three months ago, he wrote me a letter saying that he loved me, but he told me that I should forget him because he was going into battle. I have not heard from him since. I don't think I ever will. Martyrdom was his right, of course. It had always been that way, but I still haven't come to terms with it. I will one day but not just yet. He was a brave man, begum sahiba. He stood up for his beliefs. We are cowards compared to him."

Bilqis felt like saying that martyrdom did not exonerate him. He might have been brave but what right did he have to take lives? Instead, she felt nauseated, culpable for taking him from Mumtaz. Had she not threatened him with consequences and told him to leave, he might still be alive. Had she been more conciliatory and orchestrated a wedding, the present would have been entirely different. Now it was all too late.

"What will you do now?" she asked.

"I will serve you, begum sahiba, What else?"

"You have a life to live."

"There's nothing left in it."

"There is much more."

"I'd better go." Mumtaz started to leave.

"No, wait."

"Yes?"

"Will you marry?"

"Do you want me to marry?"

"I want you to be happy."

Mumtaz laughed. She looked her same young self but her manner was that of a woman twice her age. "Happy or unhappy, what difference does it make? Life is always unsatisfactory, no matter what."

The two women never discussed the matter again.

The classroom was one of the few places where Bilqis felt immune to the violence around her. When she stood in front of her students and discussed the works of Tolstoy, Hugo and Maupassant, she felt that she was transporting them to a plane of the highest order. At

times like these, she entertained great hopes and saw future poets
and thinkers among them, but sometimes the discussions descended
into politics, and then she could see their other selves, their anger
bright, their hatred clear and hard. She remembered how one of her
students explained to her that the Mohajirs had to buy guns to defend themselves from the Pathans and the Sindhis, who were armed
to the teeth. Why would the Mohajirs go unarmed?

Her troubles began after the vice chancellor announced that
supplementary examinations were to be held because someone had
leaked the engineering papers. Miscreants had been sighted selling
worked solutions for a hundred rupees in the bazaar outside the
stationer's shop. When the results appeared, twenty students scored
one hundred percent, more than forty students scored over ninety
percent and none failed. As soon as the announcement was made,
however, radical Mohajir students boycotted all classes. Excitable
young men held press conferences in which they justified the rig-
ging because they claimed that certain teachers were demanding
payoffs in return for passing Mohajir students. It was the greatest
injustice, they said. Mohajirs were just like any other ethnic group.
Why did they have to pay bribes to pass? Protests were held against
the vice chancellor, and even some teachers, afraid of being held
hostage, even spoke for the Mohajir cause.

The vice chancellor remained adamant about the reexamina-
tion. Luckily, he had the support of the chancellor, who in turn
enjoyed the support of the governor of Sindh. When protests did
not work, the students turned violent. A group of rogues smashed
the windows of the university's administration block and broke into
the bursar's office. When the police arrived, they took to their heels,
but they returned at night, beat up the security guard, broke open
the door of the deputy registrar's office and set everything on fire,
including the new sets of examination papers.

The day after the fire, five hundred armed policemen arrived in armored cars and cordoned off the campus. Lectures were held but attendance dropped by half.

Bilqis was in the common room when she heard a commotion outside. Mohajir students were throwing up a barricade with furniture plundered from the classrooms. When she went out to stop them, they told her to mind her own business. They were courteous at first, but when she refused they became surly and gathered around her. Bilqis looked at each one of them. They all had scarves wrapped around their faces.

"Who are you?" one of them demanded.

"I teach here."

"There are no teachers or students today, only Mohajirs and others," he said. "Are you a Mohajir or not?"

She searched his eyes but there was no hint of recognition. He wasn't one of her students. Nevertheless, he was a student, and students were meant to be respectful and obedient. She was seized by a momentous rage. Choking with anger, she ripped the scarf from the young man's face and slapped him hard. The student gaped at her, dumbfounded. The next moment she regretted her impulsiveness. A trickle of sweat ran down her spine as she sensed the others closing in on her. She could not imagine that they would dare touch her, but she was shocked by their wildness. They had turned into a mob, and that frightened her. Then something else attracted their attention and they stared toward the main gate. A voice called out: "The cops are coming . . ." and everyone scattered.

Bilqis heard different voices shouting in the distance. Suddenly, there were hundreds of students swarming around her, as if they had appeared out of thin air. When they started throwing rocks at the police, the policemen opened fire. Tear-gas canisters arched toward the barricade, trailing white smoke. Shots rang out. A rubber bullet droned past her head. "Go!" someone shouted to her. "Go now!" Bilqis did not know where to go. Her eyes stung. She could not see in front of her. She covered her mouth with her handkerchief, but there was a bitter taste on her tongue. She held her breath. Her throat hurt. There were people running in all directions. It was as if she were caught in a strong current that pushed her this way and that so forcefully that there was nothing she could do. A hand grabbed her by the arm and yanked her through the melee, until she was thrown against the door of the administration building. It was locked, but the staff inside saw her and pulled her in. Outside, they heard footsteps running past. Then a frightening silence. When they opened the door, the barricade was deserted. An acrid smell hung over it. The ground was covered with broken glass and there was not a soul in sight.

Bilqis was at home the next day when she got a call from the vice chancellor to say that classes had been canceled indefinitely. "They're all good students," he said. "I don't know what's come over them. I've never seen anything like this before."

Bilqis could still recall her terror and felt less sympathetic. "Well, I hate to break it to you, but students who go about smashing up the place have no hope," she said. "You might as well give monkeys china plates to eat from."

There was a grim silence. "Begum sahiba, I know that you don't mean it," said the vice chancellor. "They are not monkeys. Some of them are, yes, there will always be some, but not all of them. Most of them are good and decent young people who need teachers like you. I hope that you return when classes resume, or whenever you decide to come back. There will always be a place here for you."

When he hung up, Bilqis went upstairs to her bedroom. How was she going to spend her time, she wondered. She decided to borrow some books from the Sind Club library. As she was getting dressed, she slipped and fell on the bathroom floor. When she tried to get up, pain shot through her leg. Afraid that she had broken something, she called out for help. Mumtaz came bounding up the stairs. When she saw her mistress, her eyes opened wide, but she bit her lip and calmly set to work. She wiped the floor with a towel and brought cushions to prop up Bilqis where she had fallen. When she was satisfied that Bilqis was relatively comfortable, she rang Sikander at work and asked him to come as soon as possible.

Bilqis was in great agony at first, but the pain gradually lessened. By this time, the news had traveled and the other servants gathered, milling about downstairs and talking excitedly among themselves. Presently, they heard Sikander's car arrive outside and they lowered their voices. Hameeda opened the door and let him in.

"Good God!" he exclaimed when he saw the congregation. "Where is my sister?"

The servants all started speaking at once. They had always been in awe of the sahib, who treated them fairly and firmly, exactly as they expected to be treated. Sikander listened and smoothed his mustache with his finger. His authority was instant. When the hullabaloo died down, he marched upstairs, giving Mumtaz a nod to follow.

"My dear sister, what have you done to yourself?" he remarked when he saw Bilqis. Then he noticed her sharply bent leg, and his face tensed. "I hope you haven't broken a bone."

"I hope I haven't," Bilqis said weakly.

"Let's get you to the hospital. We're going to have to carry you down the stairs. The girl will give me a hand. Come, Mumtaz."

Very gently, Mumtaz and Sikander lifted her. Bilqis used her good leg to get up and put one arm around her brother's neck and the other around Mumtaz's. In this manner, the three of them slowly came down the stairs. One of the servants opened the front door and another rushed out to open the car door. Bilqis winced with pain as they maneuvered her into the backseat, but she kept her demeanor. As Sikander turned the key in the ignition, Bilqis wound down her window to give Hameeda instructions to carry out in her absence.

The hospital was ready when Bilqis arrived. Sikander had rung the surgeon general in advance to make sure that his sister was seen to. The doctor diagnosed a fractured kneecap but declared it was not a serious break. He expected it to heal in four to six weeks. Bilqis was wheeled into surgery for a minor operation, where a pin was inserted in the bone. She was then admitted for two days in an air-conditioned room with a telephone, a television and a nurse on round-the-clock duty. It was the most comfortable arrangement that she could have hoped for. When Samad rang and asked if he should fly over to help, she laughed at the suggestion.

"You cannot imagine how well I am being looked after," she told him. "There's nothing more you can do."

It gave her a sense of vindication that her decision to stay put was the right choice after all, even when the truth was that she had never felt so helpless in her life. There was a heavy plaster cast on her leg. She was always in discomfort, and she could move about only with the help of wooden crutches or someone holding her by the arm.

When she was discharged from the hospital, she found herself completely dependent on Mumtaz. The girl came every morning and stayed with her till night. She helped her into and out of bed. She washed her hair, changed her clothes and cut her nails. She brought her food in bed and walked her to the bathroom and back. She interpreted her needs without being asked and without expecting gratitude in return because she knew that she was only doing what Bilqis expected her to do. The gratitude was there, of course, but Bilqis didn't need to show it.

For her part, Mumtaz felt no resentment in serving Bilqis in this manner. In fact, she had never felt so close to Bilqis. When she leaned forward to wash Bilqis's face in the sink, she could see the narrow, delicate nape of her neck. She could see the calluses on the soles of her feet when she washed her, and the blue veins on the back of her hands when she cut her nails, and when she dressed her she looked at the freckles on her shoulder blades and admired the whiteness of her skin. Sometimes she could see a vein in her temples throbbing as she sat up in bed. Then she would bring her tea and a pile of books from the study to read.

Mumtaz didn't feel like a servant when she was with Bilqis, except when there were others about, and then it did not matter somehow, because she did everything mechanically. Her thoughts were her own. No one could take them from her. Her head felt clear and cool. Look at Bilqis's son, Samad, she thought. He is rich and lives abroad but he cannot be beside his mother when she is in such need. Look at Mahbano, her own sister, who talks to her only on the telephone. Bilqis was hers. She had her all to herself. This was her time.

20

MAHBANO ARRIVED AT Bilqis's house at noon. The ride from the airport had soured her mood. For an hour, the Mercedes was stuck in a gridlock near Empress Market, where a set of traffic lights had failed. A heavy downpour in the morning had transformed the city's streets into rivers. Entire roads lay flooded, cluttered with abandoned cars, the water lapping over their seats. Rickshaws and motorcycles sputtered along on the footpaths. Bus drivers, contemptuous of a lone policeman who was trying to ease their passage, were engaged in a futile contest, edging ahead inch by inch, sounding their horns.

The oppression lifted after they crossed Clifton Bridge, which marked the boundary between the city and the posh suburbs. It was a different world here. The sea breeze rustled through the palm trees that lined the broad, well-kept roads. Even the air smelled cleaner. The Mercedes took the corners easily. Its powerful engine pushed it along, as the sunshine filtered through leafy branches and fell on its hood. The curbs flashed past, painted yellow and black. The Mercedes turned into the entrance of Bilqis's house, where a large brass plate announced in big bold letters—MR H A KHAN, LLB, BARRISTER AT LAW.

Hameeda was sweeping the driveway, bent double with a thistle broom. She grinned as the car approached and opened the door, salaaming Mahbano, who smiled at her. Ancient, unchanging Hameeda. She had known her since she was a young woman but Hameeda had seemed just as old to her then as she did now. Mahbano noticed that another pair of eyes was also watching her. A little boy was hiding behind Hameeda's legs, barefoot and wearing a red shirt that had once belonged to Samad. Dark, moist eyes peered up at her.

"Is this your grandson?" Mahbano asked.

"Yes, he's mine."

"Whose son is he?"

"My elder boy's son."

"I haven't seen him before."

"You've scarcely been visiting, begum sahiba."

Mahbano was stung by the remark and the smile faded from her lips. "What's your name?" she asked the boy.

The boy fidgeted and lowered his eyes.

"Well? Won't you speak?"

"Tell the begum sahiba your name," Hameeda said.

The boy mumbled something and looked up at his grandmother.

"Do you go to school?"

The boy shook his head.

Hameeda ran her hand through the boy's black hair. "The begum is teaching him the alphabet," she said. "She buys him books from the bazaar. If she wishes it, then he'll go to school."

"And how is she?" Mahbano asked in a low voice.

The woman made a futile gesture. "She is getting better but the healing takes time. Her leg still hurts and she hasn't been sleeping that well. She wakes up at night and then she cannot go back to sleep. She sleeps badly for three or four nights, then she sleeps soundly for a night or two, then the cycle begins again. She has grown old, begum sahiba. Old age brings along its own afflictions."

Mahbano did not like Hameeda's candor—it reflected far too much familiarity with her sister. Servants were not supposed to admit knowledge of such things. They were meant to veil their gaze. They were there to serve, not to see or hear or pass opinions about their employer, least of all to their employer's sister. That was not their prerogative. And if that happened, if they dared to take such liberties and give themselves such airs, then they were obviously not being disciplined. Bilqis's notions of class were rigid. Why would she allow the boundaries to blur? Alarm bells started ringing in Mahbano's head.

"You have made it quite clear," she said. "There is no need to explain. We have all grown old and I think we all know what that means." She took out a fifty-rupee note from her purse. "Your people look after her, though?"

If Hameeda heard weakness in her voice, she let it pass. She was glancing at the money. "It's our duty," she said, her hand turning into a claw, taking the money as her rightful due. The alms were not really alms. They were a token for her abiding loyalty.

When the car engine was turned off, everything became eerily quiet. Except for the sea breeze in the trees and the faint cawing of crows, there was no sound. The driver carried Mahbano's suitcase inside, while she stood in the driveway and surveyed her surrounds. As she was about to enter the house, she noted signs of neglect. The white paint on the window frames was chipped. Weeds sprouted on the driveway and in the flower beds. There was a whiff of dung. As she peered around the corner, she saw a cow tied to a tree. It hadn't been there the last time she had visited. The servants had strung a clothesline between the perimeter walls and hung towels and bright women's clothes on them to dry. A goat was tethered to a pole. Bread crumbs soaked in milk lay scattered in the side alley. A few feet away, under the shade of the lemon tree, a cat lay sprawled while furry kittens scampered about.

The cat raised its head and watched Mahbano with its yellow-green eyes. In a corner of the garden, a clutch of hens scratched about in the dust.

Mahbano examined these details with a growing sense of dismay. Ever since Samad's wedding, she had had a feeling that Bilqis was a little lost, as if she did not quite know where or what she was meant to be. Mahbano could not understand why she wanted to stay on in Karachi. What purpose did it serve to live away from her son, when most parents lived, or at least wanted to live, near their children? The episode with her fractured kneecap was only the latest proof that her sister was living on borrowed time. With a grim face, Mahbano approached the front entrance.

Mumtaz led her into the drawing room, where the ceiling fan turned slowly and a musty smell hung over the place, lending it an immutable air. Passing through the sumptuously furnished space, Mahbano was gratified to feel continuity at last. Something in the depth of her being responded to the house each time she came here. It had always been like this, ever since she was a young woman, even before she was married. Each visit was a magical sojourn in which all her worries about the past and future fell away. Only the present remained. She was gratified to feel that sensation once again in the still and peaceful aspect of her surrounds.

Bilqis was seated on a sofa reading a book. She put down her glasses and rose with the help of a walking stick to greet her sister. They embraced and kissed each other on the cheek. Bilqis looked frail and a little paler than before, but her eyes were bright and clear, and she was as elegant as ever.

"Well, Mahbano, blessings on you!" she said, gesturing for her to sit down. "Did they give you food on the plane? I hope you did not eat it. God knows what they put in it. I would not be able to forgive myself if you fell ill. You are in my care now, even if you're here for only a day or so. Save your appetite to eat with me."

Mahbano waited for her sister to prepare two paans. She passed one delicacy to Mahbano. There was a strong trace of tobacco, lime and cardamom inside the rolled betel leaf. As the women chewed, their lips and teeth turned red.

"I see you have kittens," Mahbano said.

"They've made a home here."

"Aren't they a nuisance?"

"They're like my children. They depend on me. When they grow up they'll run away but until then they are mine."

Mahbano laughed, slurping the betel juice. She felt light-headed as the tobacco melted in her mouth. "The cow too?"

Bilqis gave her a sidelong glance. "I know what you are thinking—that I am going senile, that the servants are taking over and the place is falling apart. Well, put your mind at rest. The cow gives milk. The hens lay eggs. The servants know their place. They have their whims, of course, but I keep them in order. They do not ask for much and they're good to me. The grass has not been cut because we are fattening the goat. I am quite beyond worrying about what the place looks like. I am nearly seventy, remember? I don't give garden parties anymore. I've had my fill of society. People only disappoint you. They let you down, even if they mean well. Sooner or later something is misconstrued and there is no rapprochement and then the resentment starts to mount, little by little, until it sets hard like concrete. The only safe option is to do nothing, to sit in my room and read until there is nothing left to read."

Mahbano, who was not a reader at all, nodded absently. "You have been reading a great deal then?"

"I have a lot of time," Bilqis said. "The hours linger on, Mahbano. They beat upon me like waves. Do you know who wrote those lines? Hashmat did. I found them among his papers. I used to go to the bookshops to buy up his books because I did not want him to know that no one else was buying them. It broke my heart to see them collecting dust. I don't think he had many readers. I never told him, of course. He wasn't a bad poet. I still don't understand why he didn't make it and others did. Anyway, pay no attention to me. I am not impartial. I used to be when he was alive, but now I take his side because I understand him better. He was writing about the end. He sensed it early on."

Mumtaz appeared silently from the kitchen. Food was served, she announced. It was laid out on the dining table. She drummed her fingers on the sofa, looked at the two women and retreated the way she had come.

"Come, it's getting late," Bilqis said, rising. "The girl won't eat until we've eaten."

There were two vegetarian bhujias on the table, served with onion rings and roti. Bilqis avoided meat curries, as they upset her digestion. The dishes were garnished with coriander and mint from the garden. The sisters ate slowly, speaking in a light and lively tone that they had used with each other since childhood. When they were by themselves, there was always a great deal to talk about.

"Did you hear about Mrs. Dilshad's daughter?" Mahbano asked, referring to a girl whom Samad had turned down. "I hear that she doesn't even condescend to greet her father-in-law. She comes to his house and sits there like a queen. She makes a face if they offer her food and turns up her nose if they try to talk to her. It's terrible! I don't know what has gotten into the heads of young people these days. We weren't so rude to our elders. We wouldn't have dared."

"What does her husband say?"

"He says nothing. She's got him under the thumb."

Bilqis laughed. "How do you know all these things?"

"I just know," Mahbano said. "People tell me their secrets."

"And how's your little darling—why did she not come to see me?"

Mahbano sighed and rolled her eyes. "What can I tell you about Zainab? She sits on the fence, procrastinates and dreams. Only

God knows what's on her mind. I can tell more about her by looking at her paintings than by talking to her. Last month, she took the bus to India."

"Why didn't she fly?"

"She wanted to travel, to see things."

"Marry her off."

"I would if I could."

"Doesn't she want to marry?"

"She doesn't like any of the young men I have shown her. They're not good enough for her."

"Is there someone she likes?"

"Look, if there were someone she wanted to marry, I'd marry her off right away, but she hasn't told us about anyone. That's why I am going to do the job for her. I don't mind that. I just don't want her to keep waiting for a true love match. Years go by like this"—she snapped her fingers—"and either Mr. Right is there or he isn't. She can't wait for him to drop out of the sky."

"You know more people than anyone, Mahbano. I am sure you will find the right match."

"Well, there is someone," Mahbano said, brightening up a little. "The boy lives in London. The family is originally from Hyderabad. They migrated to England when the children were still young. He was born here, but raised over there. Although he no longer speaks much Urdu, he understands the language. The family is good, well heeled."

"What's their name?"

"Peerzada. The boy's name is Amir. I am having them investigated."

"What does he do?"

"He has just finished his engineering degree at Cambridge."

"God be praised. Hashmat would have been pleased. Does he have an income?"

"A very good one," Mahbano said. "He makes more money in one year than Shahid has made in ten."

"What about the family? Are they religious?"

"No, not very. They are like us, modern but not wholly Westernized."

"Does Shahid mind?"

"Of course not. He knows that good boys are rare."

"What about Zainab? Does she want to go overseas?"

"She hasn't said no."

"She'll have to make up her mind quickly if a proposal comes."

"I know," Mahbano said, frowning. "She can't dillydally forever. It's about time she made some decisions about her life."

"Well, it looks like everybody is going away now," Bilqis said. "Like lemmings—can you imagine? All people care about these days is whether you know someone at a foreign embassy. If you do, they are suddenly your best friends. Air Marshal Mahmood and his wife left last month."

"Really? Where to?"

"Their children are in California."

"They had a good life here," Mahbano said, shaking her head.

"A very good life. They had a gardener, a chauffeur, a chowkidar, a cook, a washerwoman, a cleaner, a sweeper and a maid. Eight servants. They had one of the largest plots of land in the whole of Clifton. It would be worth millions. Nice people, decent, lots of friends. Still they went. Sold their house and furniture to babysit their grandchildren. Isn't that something?"

"Three families from the street behind ours left for Canada this year."

"Canada is too cold."

"Oh, they'll go anywhere. There's so little here for young people to do."

"Do you think I should migrate?" Bilqis asked.

"Of course you should think about it," Mahbano said. "It would be a comfortable life in Australia."

"I have all the comforts here."

Mahbano started counting on her fingertips. "First, they have better hospitals. Second, trains and buses run on time. Third, there are no blackouts. Fourth, you can drink the tap water without thinking that you might die and fifth, there is no violence, not the same kind that we have here. You might get racist slurs, but you won't get killed in a bomb blast. You won't get shot at crossing the road. Isn't that enough?"

Bilqis looked pained. "All the more reason to go, yes, but I can still use my arms and legs. I am not an invalid, not yet. I have my uses here. I have certain prerogatives. I will be useless there. I don't want for anything. I have been there before and each time I was glad to leave. I can endure three weeks away from this place, but any more and I feel like the air has been sucked out of my lungs. I miss my garden. I miss the bazaars. I miss the smells. I even miss the sunlight shining through the windows in the morning. If I go, I will be betraying this place. I owe it something and it'd be treacherous of me to leave. I don't have the will to go."

Mahbano smiled and shook her head.

"What, you don't believe me?"

"Oh, I believe you."

"But I amuse you?"

A laugh escaped from her lips. "I think you exaggerate sometimes. You can always come back."

Bilqis looked at her with a mixture of pity and fury. "Once you go, you don't come back. Who has ever come back? No one does."

"Go for Samad's sake."

"Samad is no longer the person I thought he was or used to be."

"What do you mean?"

"I mean he is not a child anymore. He has grown up. He has his own friends, his family and his own life to get on with. I realized this for the first time this summer, and I am still coming to terms with it. When you have a child, you always want to see him reflected in the adult he becomes. It may seem a trifling matter to you, and perhaps it is, but I am only beginning to learn that it is an impossible thing to ask for. When he was a little boy, he wanted to be with me all the time. I took him with me and later he followed me everywhere, just happy to be doing things with a parent, the way small children are. That was the image that I kept in my mind, of being inseparable from him. When he went to boarding school, I saw less of him, of course, but when I did see him it was like the old times again. I cooked for him. I laid out his clothes on his bed. I looked after him. For those brief periods that he came home, he was mine. I felt that he needed me and depended on me. For me, it was as if he never grew up. I never paid any attention to his other world, the world away from home. It was like the dark side of the moon for me. I could not comprehend it because I could not believe that he could do without me. In my mind he only came to life when he was with me. I could not imagine that, one day, that other world would take him away from me. I should be happy, I know—it's hardly a misfortune to see your child busy with his own life, the very opposite, in fact, but it still hurts."

"Zainab is still a child through and through," Mahbano said.

Bilqis smiled and made a dismissive gesture with her hand. "Perhaps you are right. People never change. At least their essence never changes. What changes is time, and their relationships and their feelings about others, and who they share their thoughts with and who they cease to talk to. You may still see Zainab as a child but it may just be that she has barred you from her world and you only see what little remains of her old self. Have you ever seen her with her friends? She might be unrecognizable to you. Samad uses a different tone of voice for me than for Kate. I thought that he was a serious person who never laughed until I saw him laughing with her. I felt like saying, 'Why can't you laugh with me like that? Why can't you talk to me in that voice?' But of course, you can't say that. What right do you have to say that when you don't own them anymore?

"Time goes very quickly, Mahbano. Before you know it, the children are adults and the magical bond that you thought you had with them no longer exists. I don't mean that they don't love you—they do; one certainly hopes so; otherwise it would be very hard to live in peace with oneself—but it's not the pure love of a small child. It is a different kind of emotion, so that when they do something for you, you never know if they do so out of love or out of a sense of duty.

"I hope for your sake that I am wrong. Girls are different. Once they have their own children, they let their mothers become their friends and confidantes. With men, it is not possible. They shut you out completely. They do not understand how much we need to keep on playing the role of a parent to keep our own sense of continuity. It is pitiful, isn't it, that our own children have no place for us? Not out of their malice or rancor, but simply because that is the way of the world. That is worse than being mortal, knowing that one day you will cease to exist, not only your body but also your memory, and it will be like you were never born. That knowledge is easier to bear because we think of oblivion as part of the indefinite future and not the immediate present. Having no place in the immediate present is far worse."

"I don't think you should look for a meaning in it," Mahbano remarked. "It's not calculated or conscious, as you say. It's just what happens when children grow up. If you lived near them, you'd feel closer."

"But you can't impose yourself on them," Bilqis said. "You can't arrive with your suitcases at their doorstep and say that you'll be staying for four months. Those days are well and truly gone."

Mahbano followed her sister's digressions perfectly. "I hope you don't mind me asking this, but this is not about Kate, is it?"

"No, it's not about her. She is all right."

"She is all right, is she?"

"Why—you look surprised."

"I thought it was all about her."

"It was," Bilqis said, chuckling, "but we've made our peace."

"Have you?"

"What choice did I have?"

"You could have made her miserable."

Bilqis was startled. "Do I make people miserable?"

"Never mind."

"Have I made you miserable?"

"How do you think I felt when you didn't agree to Shahid marrying me?"

"You still haven't forgotten?"

"Of course not."

"Well, we made up. I let things go, didn't I?"

"I suppose so."

"Still uncertain?"

"No."

"Good, we move on. That was so long ago. I can't believe that you are still stewing over it."

"What about your granddaughter?" Mahbano asked. "You'd be near her. You can still make her yours."

"Ah, yes . . . Tara . . ." Bilqis's tone softened as she remembered kissing and hugging her grandchild. Her mind wandered off and she felt a desire to gaze at her in peace. "She is very young now. Who knows what she will be like when she grows up, especially if she grows up overseas? She might detest me, a foreigner. She might not want to talk to me."

"She might love you."

Bilqis stopped for a moment, as if she were hesitating to reply. "People like us don't leave. We have it good here."

"But it's not safe anymore," Mahbano said. "You know that as well as I do."

Bilqis sighed and glanced at her sister. "I am like a frog in cold water that boils to death without suffering. I am happy where I am. Even if things get difficult, what difference does it make? At my age, it's all the same. I raise the boundary walls each year and put a bigger padlock on the gate. The more lawlessness there is, the higher my wall. Life goes on, Mahbano. For me, this city is no longer a city. It is my body, my blood, my bread and my bones. I no longer see the manholes and the rubbish dumps. I no longer hear the gunshots in the night. I am oblivious to its malaise because its ailments are my own. Loyalty to a place is a strange thing. Call it my conceit, my delusion, my blindness; I suspect myself that it is lassitude, but I don't mind; there it is. Everyone knows me here. When I go to the market, I feel like I am going to another part of my house. The shopkeepers salaam me. The butcher gives me his prime cut. The baker delivers fresh bread and some nice young man always carries my groceries. I like that certainty. I have my place, and I like that. I don't wish to go somewhere new and explain to people what and who I am. I have earned my respect once. I don't wish to earn it all over again."

Mahbano looked at her sister in bewilderment. Suddenly, she seemed greatly aged. Had she completely failed to see it in the past, or had the accumulation of years suddenly crystallized? The change terrified her.

"Why this silence, Mahbano?" Bilqis remarked. "Is something the matter?"

Mahbano picked at her food. "I was thinking that soon there won't be anyone left except us old people."

"And our servants." Bilqis smiled.

"And what will become of us?"

"Why, my dear, we'll rot."

21

AUTUMN CAME WITH its deceptive chill. Bilqis was laid up with a cold as usual. Her throat had started to tickle the night before and, by the morning, her whole body ached. These colds seemed to be lasting longer and be harder to shake off every year. Even as a child, she remembered feeling a dreadful weakness that struck her just before the illness, but this time it was different—it was a gathering darkness that spread out from the pit of her stomach and extended into her limbs. She went to bed at noon to get some rest. All her senses became terribly acute. Her heart was like the beating of a drum. She drew the curtains as the daylight blinded her. The smell of a ripe banana made her sick. In the evening, she felt cold and started shivering. She covered herself with blankets and a heavy quilt. The woolen blankets rubbed like sandpaper against her skin. She went from being cold to hot to cold again. Her sheets were soaked with sweat and she started to cough. It was dawn when she finally slept.

A few hours later, she awoke with a metallic taste in her mouth. She hoped that she might feel better after breakfast and took her temperature. The mercury stood at 102.3 degrees, exactly one degree more than on the previous day. She rang the doctor. He was busy at his clinic but he came with his bag at noon. He listened to her chest and took her temperature again.

"One hundred and three point one degrees."

"Is it serious?" she asked.

"It isn't good," he replied.

"Is it flu?"

He gave her acetaminophen to bring down the fever. "We'll wait and see for a day," he said. "If you don't get better, then you'll have to go to the hospital. You might have complications."

All that day she lay in bed, coughing and shivering, her blood pounding in her ears. She had to clench her teeth to stop them from chattering. Mumtaz went in and out of her room to fetch things. The doctor came in the evening and gave her more acetaminophen. She sank into a dreamless sleep. Hameeda rolled out a mat and slept on the floor beside Bilqis's bed, constantly muttering incantations and begging God to give her the sickness that afflicted her mistress.

The next morning, the cough had worsened. Mumtaz rang Sikander, who came immediately. He drove Bilqis straight to the hospital, where a specialist X-rayed her chest and diagnosed pneumonia. She was admitted and put on intravenous penicillin. A nurse applied wet flannel packs to her forehead and feet. The fever subsided, and by afternoon Bilqis felt well enough to prop herself up in bed. Mumtaz brought her chicken soup and a bouquet of freshly cut roses from home. In the evening, she was able to receive both her siblings during visiting hours. They brought a fruit bowl and sat by her bedside, making light conversation to lift her spirits. Mahbano reminisced about the times when everyone used to go to the Pioneer Coffee House for pastries. Sikander remembered the cabarets and floor shows at the Metropole Hotel.

"I haven't the faintest notion why you prefer Rafi over Saigal," Sikander said to Mahbano. "Rafi produced reams of music and there is some very good material there, but he also sang a lot of mediocre songs. Saigal sahib's music has the divine spark, each and every piece. He sang only in his finest hour. He never wasted his energies on mediocrity, and that's the secret of his immortality."

"You're a zealot," Mahbano said.

"I am an aesthete," he replied. "I base my judgments on merit."

"All right, then, tell me if you prefer Nur Jehan to Lata? Of the two divas, who is the queen of Indian singing?"

"Lata."

"Traitor," Bilqis remarked, smiling. She was surprised to hear her own voice. It seemed raspy and unlike her. Mahbano came over and stood beside her. Bilqis could see that she had been crying a good deal.

"Samad rang," Mahbano said.

"Did you tell him?"

"Yes. He is on his way."

Bilqis groaned. "He need not come. Did you tell him that?"

"He wouldn't listen."

Bilqis let her head sink into the pillow and closed her eyes. She was calm but she felt indifferent to everything. She could not understand why everyone was so worried about her when she felt so light. The conversation of her siblings turned into a distant murmur.

When she awoke the next morning, she saw the clouds scudding across the sky from her bedside window. There was something about the angle of this perspective that reminded her of her childhood days, when she would lie on one of those old reclining wicker chairs with its legs shaped like a lion's paws, which her father had kept in their chalet in Darjeeling, and watch the clouds fly across the sky to the Himalayas, where they would bring snow. These memories became more and more vivid. Every little detail, every smell and sound began to emerge from the irretrievable past, making it seem that nothing had changed between those long-lost days and today except for a vast gulf of time that had shrunk and then disappeared altogether. A past that photographs and stories could no longer bring back to life was resurrected by her feverish mind. Doctors and nurses came and went but she paid them no heed. They no longer mattered because the souls of people she had lost long ago were here again today; they had overcome death, manifesting themselves in the scent of the earth, the limpid light and the crows cawing in the trees. The entire ether was pregnant with their presence, quivering, waiting for her to recognize them and break the spell that imprisoned them. A nurse came in and turned on the light. Bilqis asked her to turn it off and draw the curtains. She wished to rest.

The memories now started flashing past at a frantic pace. The house in Calcutta where she grew up, with its terrazzo floors and palm trees and the Eurasian governess who thought she was white, the scrawny mullah who came by on his bicycle twice a week to teach the children the Koran, the transvestite employed to teach them classical dance and the legions of fussy, elderly aunts who chewed betel leaf as they recalled the courtly times of India and told her tales of lost splendor. Tara's face floated before her eyes. She counted the months since she had last seen her and imagined what she might be doing had she remained there by Tara's side. She would be seeing her sitting up and smiling and crawling perhaps and she would be bathing her and putting her to sleep. She thought of Samad. Where was he? Why was he not here? She was sorry that she could not have been a better mother, sorry that she could not talk to him more. There were so many things that she could have told him but never did, and now they would die with her, never to be recounted again. She could not imagine that she would no longer be able to see his life unfold. It seemed so unfair. Death! It was already here. It would snatch his life from her as it would snatch hers from him. And then she no longer felt anything. She did not even know what the images represented or why they were flashing through her mind. She could no longer feel her body, but she felt an acceptance that was neither happiness nor sadness. The awareness of this state was her last thought.

PART 3

22

TARA WAS SEVEN years old when she went to Pakistan for the first time. After staying for a few days at Bilqis's house, Samad took her and Kate for a trip to Murree. Tara had no memory of her grandmother and she had never seen her house, but she loved Murree. It was one of the girl's happiest memories of her visit. The family went on walks every day, meandering along the deserted roads, the hills coiled around them like the graves of buried leviathans, the air rustling through the pines. They would follow a goat path and come upon a meadow full of daisies and blue gentians, nestled among the oaks and the chestnut trees, and there they would spread out their red picnic blanket on the grass and eat their sandwiches with steaming tea from a thermos. The visit filled her with a sensation of quiet, idle enchantment that stayed with her even after she returned to Karachi.

Bilqis's house was to be sold. The family had vacillated about its fate. It was Samad's inheritance, and he would have sold it long ago but for Mahbano, who wanted him to keep it for family reunions. Sikander suggested tenants, but good tenants were difficult to come by, and the family, despite promises renewed every year, never managed to gather together. Meanwhile the house was left empty.

Samad decided to sell it before the place became derelict, and came to oversee the settlement. As the day of the sale approached, he felt an increasing sense of discomfort. It was odd because he had felt nothing when his mother died. He had rehearsed her death a thousand times. He had imagined how the telephone would ring, how he would have to pack his suitcase and make his way on a hastily booked flight home. He had gone over each detail of that trip, and indeed, when Sikander rang him to say that Bilqis was unwell, he felt exactly as he had imagined he would, like a well-rehearsed actor who was going through the motions. He was stoic, his eyes dry, his heart like stone. She was alive when he boarded the plane but she was dead when he arrived. That was how he had always expected it to end, abruptly and without atonement.

For years, he went on living in the belief that he was the victim of her wrongs. He felt angry that by refusing to live with him she had denied him the only path he could take to placate his conscience. He felt resentful that she had not made peace with him. These were his main emotions, not regret. This notion of wrong endured rendered him immune from grieving. Regret touched him when the furniture began to disappear. As the chandeliers, the gilt-edged mirrors, the books and the cabinets were loaded on trucks and taken away, he felt that someone was tearing the flesh from his body. It was then that he realized how much his feelings and memories were part of the house, a place that he had always imagined he would be able to come back to. A future in which it was no longer part of his life was much harder to contemplate.

One night, Sikander dropped by with a take-out meal that he had picked up on his way back from work. They mustered together some plates and cutlery from the kitchen and sat down to eat. Everything tasted good—the biryani, the kebabs, the ice cream; even the Coca-Cola tasted better in the hot weather. Conversation was muted and pleasant.

"What came after dinosaurs?" Sikander quizzed Tara. The girl was perched on Samad's knee.

"Apes."

"And what came after apes?"

"People?"

"That's right."

"Did God create people?"

"Of course."

"And who created God?"

Sikander laughed and glanced at the child's parents. "Who do you think?"

"I don't know," the girl said. "You tell me."

"Well, I don't know either. I don't think anyone does."

Tara slid off her father's knee and started rolling a pair of dice on the floor.

"She asks hard questions," Sikander remarked. "I wonder who she takes after."

"Her mother, no doubt," Samad replied.

"I think it might be her grandmother, actually. She's an inquisitor, just like her."

Kate cleared the table. The two men rose and seated themselves in the drawing room. Samad offered him a box of mint chocolates. A few minutes later, Kate emerged from the kitchen and joined them.

"What happened to the servants?" she asked.

"Missing them, are you?" Sikander joked. "They stayed on to look after the house, but there was nothing left for them to do. After a couple of years, they left. Hameeda returned to Attock with her husband. Her younger son still lives in Karachi, but the elder went to Lahore with his family and the two sisters. Mumtaz married her cousin. Mahbano paid for the dowry out of Bilqis's estate, leaving enough for her younger sister as well, who now works for her. Mumtaz's husband works on an oil rig in the Persian Gulf."

"I wonder how she is," Kate remarked.

"She is a mother now, I hear. Her husband sends her enough money so she doesn't have to work. The day is not far when she'll have her own servants and her own house. You liked her, didn't you? My sister told me so. Well, I am sure she'd be delighted to have you over for a cup of tea."

Night fell. After Kate and Tara went upstairs to bed, the electricity went out. Blackouts were common now. Samad lit some candles and put them up on the piano. Their flickering light threw long shadows on the walls. When the two men were alone, conversation turned to Bilqis.

"We had no warning that she was going to die," Sikander said. "She looked well. I have seen her looking worse. She was fine as far as I could tell, but the truth is that you could never tell with her what she felt like. Sometimes she looked radiant while being very sick and other times she looked ghastly without there being anything wrong with her. She was different in her old age, you see. You probably did not notice because you weren't here. There was a certain fatalism in her mood that was new. She was on an even keel, more detached and aloof than she used to be. She didn't get worked up about things anymore, at least not as much as she used to. I don't even think that the university riots upset her. It was as if she were expecting them all along. When she fell and fractured her kneecap, she was a little off-color, of course, but I felt that she accepted misfortunes more readily. She was resigned to them. It was not that she had become apathetic or lost her courage. I think she just ran out of steam. She had a strong constitution, but for years, I think, ever since Hashmat passed away, she was running on empty. She did not like to show weakness. She liked people to think that she was strong. The pretense of strength sapped her."

"The house has not changed," Samad remarked. "It is as I remember it, every bit of it."

"What do you mean?"

"I mean that it is hard to believe that she has been gone for years when everything else is the same."

"Except that we've all grown older," Sikander replied. "I remember when you were a child and you sat on that sofa, you used to wear shorts and your feet did not touch the ground. How long ago was that? It seems like last year, or the year before or perhaps five years ago, not thirty. Memory is a sieve. We only remember the things that keep us sane."

He rose and went to a cabinet against the wall. He poured himself a scotch from a decanter.

"A wonderful thing, drink. The harder it is to get, the more you enjoy it. It's like that with everything. Surfeit numbs the senses and scarcity heightens them. I have a good bootlegger. His brother, father and uncle are all in the business. I pay him well. He keeps his commission and gives the rest to the police. I know it's all a bit wrong, but it keeps everyone happy."

Samad laughed. He was pleased to see his uncle. His tall frame was slightly bent, but there was something youthful about him. His hair was combed back, revealing a high, boyish forehead. It was not difficult to imagine him as a handsome young man.

"Would you like me to fix you one?"

Samad shook his head.

"You don't drink?"

"Not tonight."

Sikander put the decanter away and went back to his chair. "Suit yourself," he said. "I want you to be at your ease. After all, I don't see you enough, and the times we see each other are all too brief for formality."

"Why did she not migrate?" Samad asked.

"Pride," Sikander said. "Your mother did not migrate out of pride. We have lived a life that is rooted in centuries of experience, and there is a sense of continuity here that is not easy to break. She belonged here. That's the reason she never left."

"I wish I had come back."

"She would not have wished it."

"Why?"

"There was a time when Karachi was a city open to the world. There was life here. A fellow could order a Chateaubriand on Victoria Road, wash it down with a fine Bordeaux and be at the Beach Luxury in time to watch cancan girls while an Italian orchestra played tunes from *Orpheus in the Underworld*. For young men like me—I was young once—the conundrum was whether to feast one's eyes on a continental blonde singing 'Alma Llanera' or enjoy watching a classical dancer like Panna. Lost! Lost! Casinos, bars and dance halls! All forever gone. This is a very different place. It is as if we erased everything that was good and pleasant and civilized about ourselves and started again with the negative of it all. The country you grew up in no longer exists. It's long gone. Zia destroyed it. The institutions are gone. The bureaucracy is broke. Petty officials make arbitrary rules and send people on wild-goose chases. People want dignity and respect and what they get is a life in hell. I cannot even renew my license without parting with a little bribe. Even paying a bill is a nightmare. People are turning to the religious parties out of despair. Faith is their last hope. It's like going to the quack after the doctor lets you down. If you had nothing to lose and someone told you that he had the panacea, then you'd be tempted too. We would have liked you to live here, but you would have suffered. You wouldn't have had as good a life as we did. This democracy we have is a sham. Benazir is in power but she is just clinging by her fingernails. Zia might be dead but others will take his place. The grain of the place is turning against us. Only the military and Islamists have any real power and they are not like us. No one likes to send his children away, but that's why we sent you away. We don't belong here."

"You are still here."

Sikander laughed and paused to light a cigarette. "We did what we thought best. We made choices for you, but God knows if we made the right ones. Maybe we should have let you make your own choices. The world is certainly a different place now from what it was ten or fifteen years ago, but who could have foreseen it? I still think you are better off there than here. Things will only get worse here, but don't get me wrong. I know what you mean."

Sikander swallowed the last drop in his tumbler. Rivulets of sweat glistened in the deep lines of his face. He dried his neck with a handkerchief and looked at his nephew. There was a long silence.

"Your mother had the same hopes of any mother," he said. "There are many things that she would have preferred, but she also knew a mother's fate. She came to terms with life. You couldn't have redeemed yourself by staying here or by taking her away, so don't feel culpable. Don't martyr yourself with the notion that you are guilty for not fulfilling your filial obligations. She never demanded a reckoning. You were exonerated from those duties. For better or worse, she set you free."

Tears were running down Samad's face. It did not matter what his uncle said and thought. All that mattered now was his inner dialogue, the silent explanation that he was going to provide to the inquisitor within, whose judgment was final.

23

After his uncle left, Samad was unable to sleep. A great sorrow was breaking him into pieces. Sorrow for time lost; sorrow for always wanting to be elsewhere, for attempting to live two lives at the same time; sorrow for feeling that the real conversation, the real thing, lay around the corner; sorrow for trying to capture time and having lost it entirely. He lay in bed, tossing and turning, his eyes wide open, his mind racing with thoughts. His wife lay next to him, fast asleep. They had been together nearly ten years, but it seemed to him that he had been sleepwalking all this time. He remembered their time together but he could not recall experiencing anything. It was like having someone else's memories. Things became clear only when he went back twenty or thirty years. They assumed a vividness then, as if only those long-gone years had any value and everything since then had been a waste.

He sat up in bed with his back to Kate. He waited for her to rouse, but she remained asleep, her breathing undisturbed. As he started to put on his shoes, she woke up.

"What are you doing?" she asked.

"Nothing."

"Are you going somewhere?"

"I am going for a walk."

"What's wrong?"

"Nothing."

She drew closer. "Are you sad?" she asked.

"A little."

"Come lie with me," she said.

Samad shook his head. "I can't sleep."

"Just lie down for a bit."

Samad lay down with his shoes on, thinking how much their relationship had changed. There was a time when he slept better alone in a separate bed. Now he needed her by his side to go to sleep. He ran his fingers through her hair. He knew its smell, its texture. Was it a natural evolution, a matter of becoming familiar with another person, or was it that other, damnable thought that had taken root in his mind? Had his mother's death brought them closer?

"I have to go," he said, rising.

"What time is it?"

"It's late."

"Is it safe?"

"I'll be all right."

Kate watched him leave. He paused outside the room where his daughter was asleep, deliberating whether he should go in to look at her. He loved her dearly. Nothing mattered to him more than her well-being and happiness. The sight of her small body would soothe him, and send him back to bed. His heart felt light and then heavy again. He very nearly turned the door handle, but then he changed his mind. He went downstairs and walked out the door.

Outside the house, he lit a cigarette and started the long walk toward Saddar, where the tea shops did a brisk night trade. A few rickshaws sputtered past him but he wanted to walk, as if on a pilgrimage.

He remembered the night that he stormed out of his mother's study. It was a night like tonight, the air warm and humid.

After nearly an hour he found himself outside the walls of the Sind Club. He walked past the Art Deco façade of the Metropole Hotel and the dark spires of the Holy Trinity Cathedral that rose behind a cluster of expensive carpet shops. AMERICAN EXPRESS ACCEPTED HERE said the stickers on their windows. He crossed an intersection at the traffic light and went down Abdullah Haroon Road, along the rear wall of the Press Club. Every lane here, every street, bore a memory from his boyhood. On his right lay the labyrinthine Zainab Market. Its shops had closed their shutters hours ago. Across the intersection of Inverarity Road, which had changed its name to Sarwar Shaheed Road, rose the cupola and balcony of one of the last remaining buildings from the Raj. It stood there like a proud watchman from the past. Samad stared at its pale yellow stone, which glowed in the dim light of the streetlamps. It was like a kindred soul, melancholic and out of place in the order of the present day.

Walking and smoking, he made his way toward Empress Market. In one of the tea shops, he sat down at an empty table and ordered a pot of tea. The walls were painted mustard, the tables dark wood. It was the sort of place, populated by insomniac journalists and old Communists, where decor and appearances had ceased to matter. Long ago he would have looked down on it, but tonight he was pleased to be there. He looked at the other people but nobody recognized him. No one even gave him a second glance. They were complete strangers. The animate past, the vibrant and soulful past, the past with its essence of immediacy intact, no longer existed. It had ceased to be.

"Watermelon?" someone asked.

Samad looked at the small boy who had materialized beside him. He was five or six years old, bare feet, but he had the wizened eyes of an adult. The waiter shooed him away. Samad had never felt pity for beggars before, considering them pests. Now a veil lifted from his eyes and he saw human beings. Things that had always been part of his consciousness suddenly bothered him. Sights that he had taken for granted seemed alien. He picked up a newspaper. There were cartoon strips and an editorial about a new pop-music program on television. The stock market was doing well. Property prices were rising. Everything seemed normal. Its ordinariness made it remarkable. Who could have thought five years ago that the generals and soldiers would disappear overnight? Who could have imagined that the country would turn around so quickly as to become almost unrecognizable? There was something glacial, terrifying and indifferent in this passing of time. It was like a sign, saying that this was no longer his time and place, that coming here was a transgression he ought not to have allowed himself. Where, then, was *his* time and place? Was that not the question? He gulped down the tea and headed out once again into the street.

Sometimes he had dreams of oblivion. In one dream, he saw faces of people he was supposed to know, except that he no longer remembered their names, who they were and what they meant to him. In another dream, he rang up friends he had grown up with only to discover that strangers picked up the phone. To live happily anywhere, one must make one's peace with the place, and he had never made his. Living abroad had not suited him at a deeper, more profound level. There was a boredom in it, a dullness and blandness that rendered it into a ghostly half-life, of no consequence. Only when he returned to his own country did he feel his dormant powers awakening again; the dullness left him and the warm, dry air heightened his senses, loosened his tongue and revived him.

"Tiger, tiger, burning bright . . ." Blake's poem was one of the first English verses that he had learned at school, and tonight it echoed in his mind just as it used to when he had memorized it. To live, to really live, one must struggle. One must live in the midst of struggle, in white heat. The life that Samad had lived was a good life, a superior life, but it was a life without soul. That was not how he was meant to have lived it. The friends he had left behind—the same people who had once envied him for going away—had families, houses and servants to show for themselves. Somehow, miraculously, they had endured, and made it, while his own departure now seemed Pyrrhic and hollow. His house was more beautiful than theirs. He had more money than they did, but they seemed happy, and that spoke to him of his defeat. Was there anything he could have done to change the course of things? Had he never left, had he stayed by his mother and married into society, then perhaps his remorse would have been less, though God knew what other cause for rancor he might have found then.

It was nearly three o'clock when he started walking home. His feet ached. When he became tired, he sat down by the side of the road. He had never seen the city at this time of night. It seemed so peaceful. The air was still, like water at the bottom of a well. There was some traffic on the roads but it was no longer threatening and seemed almost plaintive. When a car drove past, the silence drowned out its noise. He smoked cigarette after cigarette until he had emptied his pack. When he crossed Clifton Bridge, the stars were vanishing from the night sky.

He entered the house and left his shoes at the door. He went barefoot into the drawing room, opened the french doors out to the veranda and stood for a while in the dark, listening to the sound of crickets in the garden. He caught sight of the moon behind a trail of blue, wispy clouds. In a few hours it would be daylight. He went to the kitchen and poured himself a glass of cold water, then went into the study, turned on the lamp and slumped on the couch. The bookshelves were empty. The carpet had been rolled up and put to one side against the wall. The floor had been washed and swept clean.

In the bare space, Samad saw a crate full of little pieces of chinoiserie, empty boxes of Cohibas that his father had smoked, boxes containing ten- and twelve-inch gramophone records with the orange HMV label: Wilhelm Furtwängler and Frank Sinatra; operas by Cordillo; Maria Callas and De Curtis.

Underneath them were tapes of duets by Ustad Vilayat Khan and the shehnai maestro Ustad Bismillah Khan. They were his mother's favorites. Next to these was a pile of letters, preserved because they had caused her sorrow or joy. Underneath the pile was a striking black-and-white photograph of a young woman in a wedding dress. She was wearing a dark gharara, cut with trimmings of gold around the edges. The sleeves were tight; the folds of frock that began at her midriff flowed down to her feet. Her slender hands were dyed with beautiful patterns of henna. She held them outward. Her dark, almond-shaped eyes sparkled in her fine-boned face. Samad was startled by the image—his mother when she was young.

There were times when he had wished her dead. It was never a true wish, never malicious, only a passing, half-crazed whim that lasted no more than a second, but the thoughts and actions of a man are more inseparable than he thinks, and even those unutterable thoughts that are never put into deeds take hold of and shape one's fate. If she would not come to him, then only by dying could she liberate him and grant him the peace he so desperately craved, but now that he had got his wish, there was no peace at all. Now he knew, and the truth was that he had always known, that for all her faults, she had loved him.

It was an abstract kind of love, not practical, not spoken, not demonstrable and without proofs, but it was always there. Even if

she had hated or resented something he had done, she had loved
him all the same. It was he who had kept her at a distance. He had
resented her rigidness and her opinions. He had blamed her for no
longer listening. He had thought that she had become oblivious of
change when in fact it was he who had become indifferent; he who
had shown her no empathy; he who had made up his mind; he who
had failed to communicate, to understand and to reconcile. He had
perceived things that did not exist. His mother had held no grudges.
She was not his enemy; he was. His suffering was his own inven-
tion. If there was anyone to blame, it was him. He was the villain.

It was eight o'clock when Samad awoke. He had fallen asleep on
the couch. The sun was already high in the sky. He could hear the
sound of the piano in the next room. His daughter was playing. He
imagined the scene—the little girl perched on a stool, playing with
one hand, while her mother stood beside her, proud of the child's
ability. She gave little concerts at home for the family, where everyone sat around the piano and clapped at the end of each piece.
Sometimes she played the keys randomly, but even then there was a
certain virtuosity, a bell-like harmony in her improvisations that
conveyed her innate musical sense.

When he went into the drawing room, the scene was just as he
had imagined. His beloved child was sitting there. Her arms were
brown from the sun. She closed the piano and returned to the dining room, where she had been having breakfast. Samad watched for
a few moments as she munched on a piece of toast. Then he crossed
the room and sat down next to Kate.

"Well, there's your father, Tara," she said. "What did you want
to tell him?"

"I saw Grandma last night," she said.

"In a dream?" Samad asked.

"No, it wasn't a dream. I was awake. She came into my room. She came to me."

"Your grandma died when you were a baby. You understand that, don't you?"

"I do."

The curtains had been taken down from the windows. The sun bathed everything in a bright, blinding light. Sunlight fell on the table. Particles of dust hung in the air. Samad felt like he was seeing things for the first time, as if the whole world had been washed clean. Suddenly he realized that his mind was at rest. Something deep inside him had been released. He felt a sense of completeness, an almost divine feeling of love and acceptance. Tara looked at her father with big, solemn eyes. She doted on him. She felt that she had told him what he needed to know. Everything was still, everything silent. And then she saw him smile.

Passarola Rising

ISBN 978-0-14-303861-0

PENGUIN
BOOKS

In the year 1731, Alexandre Lourenco watches as his brother Bartolomeu's airship, the *Passarola*, ascends from St. Jorge's Castle in Lisbon. Together the brothers embark on a journey that will take them from the salons and bordellos of Enlightenment Paris to the far reaches of the North Pole in search of scientific knowledge. As they encounter such characters as the loquacious Voltaire and the irascible King Stanislaus of Poland and attempt to escape Russian enemy fire and the condemnation of Portugal's Cardinal Conti, Alexandre hopes to find his calling in life, while Bartolomeu keeps his eyes on the *Passarola*'s next horizon.